I0720252

IN THE FRAME

David Bradwell

IN THE FRAME

In The Frame is the novella prequel to the Anna Burgin series of mystery thrillers, and introduces Anna and journalist Danny Churchill.

Photography student Anna Burgin didn't expect to be arrested, but she's the only suspect for a series of crimes, and the Police have found damning evidence in her room.

But Anna has no recollection of doing anything wrong. Was it a moment of madness? Or is somebody setting out to destroy her?

And is the stranger in the bar really trying to help, or just part of an evil conspiracy?

ABOUT THE AUTHOR

David Bradwell grew up in the north east of England but now lives in Letchworth Garden City in Hertfordshire. He has written for publications as diverse as Smash Hits and the Sunday Times and is a former winner of the PPA British Magazine Writer of the Year Award. Aside from writing, he runs a hosiery company with web sites at www.stockingshq.com and www.tightsandmore.com.

Get in touch at:
www.davidbradwell.com

IN THE FRAME

The Series Prequel Mystery Novella - Anna Burgin Book 3

In The Frame was first published in 2018 by Pure Fiction
Copyright © David Bradwell, 2018
www.davidbradwell.com

ISBN: 978-1-9997099-7-6

All rights reserved. No part of this publication may be reproduced, stored or transmitted in any form by any means, electronic, mechanical, photocopying or otherwise, without prior written permission.

The right of David Bradwell to be identified as Author of this work has been asserted by him in accordance with the Copyright, Designs and Patents Act, 1988 This is a work of fiction. Names, places, events and incidents are either the products of the author's imagination or used fictitiously. Any resemblance to actual persons, living or dead, or actual events is purely coincidental.

For Carrie

A note from Anna

I didn't ever want to mention this again. I wanted to put it behind me, and pretend it never happened. But Danny finally persuaded me. He said it might help. Please don't judge me. I'm not a bad person, whatever anyone else may tell you. And if you can give me that at least, then maybe we can agree that this should never be discussed again.

PROLOGUE

Tuesday, November 21st, 1989

OBVIOUSLY, having £10,000-worth of the polytechnic's stolen photographic equipment hidden at the bottom of my wardrobe wasn't wise, but I didn't think the police would find it. That's why I was happy to allow them to search my room. Maybe, in retrospect, that was an error.

I hadn't planned on spending my morning being arrested. I wasn't surprised it happened, though, especially given the overwhelming evidence against me. As the detective was keen to stress, I'd been caught red-handed.

"You were the only person in the photographic department last night," he said, "so the only person on the planet with the opportunity."

And as for a motive? I was a student, so short of cash for drugs. What's a little bit of robbery when you have a violent dealer to pay?

Then, of course, there was the physical proof. I had the stolen goods in my possession.

"Has anybody else had access to your room since last night?" he asked.

"No," I said. "Definitely not."

There was no possible defence.

I was taken away for further questioning, much to the voyeuristic delight of my housemates, who seemed disproportionately beguiled by my state of discomfort. I tried to protest my innocence, of course, but even I had to admit that it was a cut-and-dried case. Bang to rights. An easy one for the jury. Throw away the key.

I pictured the headlines: "Photography student Anna Burgin destroys glittering future in bungled Polytechnic heist." Not, really, my finest moment, but there was worse to come. Much worse. At the station I was informed that they knew exactly what I'd been up to. The robbery had been definitively linked to similar thefts from other locations over recent months. All were likely to be added to my list of charges. Protesting was pointless.

I imagined the horrified look on my mother's face when I returned to Manchester in disgrace - assuming I could somehow avoid the extra ignominy of a prison sentence. She'd always wanted me to get a proper job, never been keen on me moving to London to pursue my passion for photography, and had warned about the dangers of the big city. She told me I'd be throwing my life away when I was consumed by the capital's darker underside. I didn't know which was worse: the end of my liberty or the smug look of told-you-so when she heard the news.

But here's the thing. I've never taken drugs. I don't have a violent dealer to pay. I didn't think the police would find the equipment because I didn't know it was in there. I'd never seen it before, and despite the compelling evidence to the contrary, the robbery really wasn't me. I just didn't have the first idea how to prove it.

Chapter 1

Two years earlier

LIKE most young boys, Danny Churchill had always been fascinated by cars, but he never thought he'd be involved in making them. He had big plans to be famous by the time he was twenty. The job at Sunderland's Nissan car plant would give him security for the next two years.

He had it all planned out. Songs written, album titles decided. He'd even designed a progression of labels that would appear on the centre of the vinyl, changing colour and theme as the band's logo evolved. He'd prepared what he'd say in interviews, and envisaged every major TV appearance, from Saturday Superstore to Juke Box Jury and beyond.

The concept was simple but he knew it would work. At sixth form, he'd persuaded his friend Chris to come on board. Danny would do all the music, Chris all the singing. Danny would stand looking all moody and mysterious, behind a bank of ever-more-impressive keyboards, while Chris would be the engaging front man. The band's name was Flag Day, and Danny planned to bedeck the stage with flags of various colours, adding vibrancy and movement and a clear visual identity. He was pretty sure he had it made.

The Nissan job gave him the money he needed to buy the equipment. Every new synthesiser, sequencer or drum machine would help move Flag Day ever closer to their ultimate destiny.

The summer of 1987 was filled with great optimism. Danny's girlfriend, Kate, helped to arrange gigs in pubs and live music venues throughout the north east. They played the Riverside in Newcastle on a battle of the bands night, although their synth-heavy electronica was not quite what the audience was used to. By the autumn they were rehearsing hard, and Danny booked a studio for two days to record four tracks for a demo tape. It was expensive but he was sure it would be worth it.

And that's when it all went wrong.

The studio days were long and demanding, and the band overran its allotted hours, before having the chance to make a final mixdown. Faced with the choice of a bigger bill or a demo that didn't do them justice, Danny opted for the former, even though it would mean selling one of his most valuable keyboards to fund it. It was a high price to pay, and made higher still the following day when Chris announced he was leaving to join a more conventional rock band. He took Kate with him.

It was a depressing situation, but there was no time to mope. Danny had two weeks to pay the studio, so advertised the synthesiser for sale in his local newspaper. A man called and said he'd buy it, and made arrangements for collection later that day. He didn't turn up. He rang to apologise, explaining that he'd been involved in a minor car crash and wouldn't now be able to proceed with the purchase.

"Sorry, mate," he said, "but I can do you a favour. My day job is the manager of Rock World in Newcastle. Do you know it?"

"Of course. I bought a drum machine from you," said Danny.

"Excellent. Well if it helps I can put the keyboard in the shop for you, and when we sell it, we'll give you whatever it goes for. No commission."

Grateful for the second chance, and with no other buyers on the horizon, Danny took the keyboard to the shop and was given a receipt. He called a couple of days later and was told there'd been a lot of interest and he should ring back after the weekend. On the Monday, Rock World went out of business. The keyboard was nowhere to be seen. But because he'd been given a shop receipt, Danny had unwittingly relinquished any claim against the manager and was instead an unsecured creditor of a failed business with masses of debt. He'd get nothing.

So, he lost the singer, the girlfriend, the band and the keyboard, and worse still, the studio was still chasing for payment. More equipment had to go. It was heartbreaking. He was back beyond square one. The police were completely uninterested in the shop manager's scam. It was a terrible injustice, but it sparked something within him: an urge to keep others from falling victim to similar schemes, and a desire to help expose those who perpetrate them. He didn't realise it then, but his destiny was sealed.

And that night, on the BBC Nine O'Clock News, he saw a report that would change his life forever.

Chapter 2

The morning before: Monday, November 20th, 1989

I QUITE like Mondays. I like the sense of the new and the feeling that things are back underway after the weekend hiatus. I suspect it would be different if I had the drudgery of commuting to an office job, but all I have to do is take pictures and immerse myself in the writings of Roland Barthes, Jacques Derrida and Sigmund Freud. Aside from occasional lectures and seminars, I'm free to set my own agenda. I know it won't last forever, but I'm determined not to get sidetracked by the constant protests and student strikes, and to make the most of my final two years. After that, who knows?

Hopefully I'll pursue a career in photography. There's a privilege and responsibility in capturing a single moment from the timeline of an infinite universe. It's insignificant in cosmic terms, and yet a single split-second frame can inspire, provoke, or even change the course of history.

But while I study hard, and I've opened my mind to new ways of thinking, a part of me is still the teenage girl who grew up in Manchester, drinking Country Manor and Diamond White when I should have been at home studying for my failed Religious Studies O Level. I live in central London, sharing the eighth floor of a hall of residence in Marylebone Road with seven others. None of us have much money, but we know how to have a good time.

I spent Sunday with my boyfriend, Todd, helping to clean up the eighth floor common room after a particularly lively party. He'd seemed a bit stressed all weekend, and the hangover wasn't helping. By the time afternoon came, and he returned home to Swiss Cottage, I set about planning my week and then tried to recharge with a very early night.

Monday morning is a good time to stay home and focus on theory. After several hours of isolation, dissecting the semiotics of cigarette and alcohol advertising, looking for the hidden messages within, I skipped lunch to start reading about the seventeenth-century Rosicrucian movement. I'm researching synaesthesia and the links between music and colours. Time can slip away when I'm concentrating. When the knock at the door came, I realised I'd missed tea too.

"Hi," I said. "What's up?" It was Amelia, my glamorous half-Japanese neighbour.

"Just checking you're all right," she said. "We haven't seen you all day."

I nodded in the direction of the textbooks, laid out across my desk.

"I've been productive." I smiled. I was pleased with my progress.

"Well done, but you look like you need a break. We're going out for dinner if you'd like to join us? Bring Todd if you like."

And that's why, just past 8pm, I was trying to decipher a menu, seated at a circular table in the window of a Chinese restaurant near Leicester Square, with Todd on one side, Amelia on the other, and three more from my hall of residence (Sophie, Sara and Meirion - our token big, blond, rugby-playing

Welshman) opposite. Amelia's jovial Cornish boyfriend, Allen with an e, made up the numbers. The alcohol and generally good-natured conversation was flowing. Meirion was proudly boasting of his leading role in the previous week's strike against student loans.

"Philosophers have only interpreted the world. The point is to change it," he said, repeating the slogan from the Student Union's banner.

"What is it this week?" asked Allen. "Loans again? Or cuts?"

"Or apartheid?" added Sara, through a cloud of hand-rolled cigarette smoke.

"Loans again," said Meirion. "I take it all you bastards will be joining the march on Wednesday?"

"I'm in," said Sara. The rest of us tried not to catch his eye. We all broadly agreed with the causes, but we weren't quite as militant in our actions.

"You bunch of bloody lightweights," he said, when nobody else answered.

"Speak for yourself," said Sara. "I did the South African Airways sit-in."

"Well I'm bloody proud. And bollocks to the rest of you."

I zoned out as the conversation turned to the current catering crisis and censorship of the reporting of events from Northern Ireland. I felt Todd's hand under the table, edging under the hem of my skirt.

"I'm so glad you could come," I said, turning and leaning into him. "It's a political madhouse. Are you not drinking?"

"No, I brought the car," he replied, in his distinctive Scouse accent. "I was hoping you might come back with me."

Todd had invested the proceeds of his part-time bar job in a secondhand Vauxhall Astra. It was a real bonus at times, as I've never got on with the Tube. I sighed.

"I'd love to, but alas not tonight. I'm so sorry. I can't stay out long. I've got an early start tomorrow. I want to crack the Rosicrucians by lunchtime."

"I can have you back before daybreak."

"And I need another good night's sleep!" I laughed. "Maybe tomorrow, though?"

"Can't. I'm working the next three nights. The weekend then?"

"It's a deal. Looking forward to it already."

Across the table, the conversation turned to a forthcoming Anti-Fascist Action benefit gig. Allen whispered something to Amelia. I followed their eyes to Meirion and Sara, who were getting on as well as usual. We'd all thought they were going to get together, but he had a girlfriend from Wales who came to stay occasionally, and to his credit he was always faithful. As far as I knew, anyway. When he wasn't flying the red flag, he played bass in a rock band, and Sara seemed to be his biggest fan. He was pouring wine with all the subtle finesse of a chimpanzee wearing boxing gloves.

The starters arrived and the conversation and debate got louder, intermingled with much laughter at the various anecdotes of brushes with authority. I could see disapproving looks from diners at a couple of the other tables, but I was powerless to lower our volume. But then I noticed that Sophie seemed unusually quiet. I leaned forward.

"Are you okay?" I asked. She looked pale. I noticed she hadn't touched her food, and her glass was still full. I knew Sophie well, as she was on my course, although she'd taken a couple of years off after school before joining and so was slightly older than me. She was normally the vivacious one, with her dyed red hair and hand-customised outfits. It was unlike her to shun alcohol.

"I don't feel too good, actually," she replied.

"That's not good. Is there anything I..."

She cut me off, excused herself, then stood up and headed

towards the front door and out into the street. The others looked up, concerned, but I said I'd follow.

"Sorry, I just needed to get some air," she said when I joined her. "It seemed so hot in there. I thought I was going to throw."

"Can I get you something? A glass of water?" I asked.

"No, I'll be fine. I just need a moment. A few deep breaths. You go back in. I'll be okay."

She didn't look okay and I wasn't going anywhere.

After a few minutes Todd came to join us. He's about 6'2" so nearly a foot taller than me. I was aware we looked slightly odd when standing next to each other.

"Can I do anything?" he asked. He'd brought my leather jacket, which was thoughtful, but I wrapped it round Sophie. She was shivering.

"I think I ought to be getting home," she said. "I'm so sorry."

"Hey, don't worry. I'll come with you."

She shook her head.

"No. I'm okay. I'll just get a cab. Thank you, though."

I looked at Todd.

"I've got my car," he said. "I'll give you a lift back."

"No, seriously, you two go back in and enjoy the night. I'll be okay. I'll just... Oh God."

She didn't look well at all. I turned to Todd. If she wasn't going to accept the offer, I'd take it up on her behalf.

"I think that would be an excellent idea, if you're sure," I said. He nodded, popped back into the restaurant to get his keys and jacket, then set off to get the Astra.

"Thanks, Anna," she said when it was just the two of us. "I just feel so guilty. I haven't felt great all day. I shouldn't have come."

"Don't be daft, these things happen. We'll get you back in no time."

"I can't ask you to come too. You haven't eaten all day."

"It's fine. It's a mercy mission."

She looked at me.

"Seriously. You stay. I'll be all right. Honestly. If Todd's happy to take me back, that'll be brilliant, but you stay with the others. I don't want to ruin it for everyone."

I tried to protest, but she was insistent.

"There's one thing you could do for me, though, if you don't mind," she said, as the car approached. "I hate to ask, but I can't see me getting in tomorrow."

"Anything you need, it's yours."

She closed her eyes for a moment, and leaned against the wall. Todd stopped beside us, hazard lights flashing. I held her arm and waited for her to speak.

"Go on," I said when she didn't say any more.

"Sorry. You'll hate me, but I've got some books and files in my locker. If I give you my key, could you pick them up for me on the way back tonight? I'm going to need them tomorrow. Stick them in a bag. There should be an empty rucksack in there. Sam's on security, I think. He'll let you in if you smile at him, but if not, don't worry."

"Of course, no problem. Give me the key and I'm on it."

She managed a smile.

"Thank you. That'll save my life. Drop them off when you get back if that's okay. I may be asleep, but if not I'll leave my door slightly open. I may still be up."

I went inside to get her coat. She told me the number of her locker and gave me the key, then Todd helped her into the car.

"There's not much point in me coming back," he said. "You'll be nearly finished. I'll drop Sophie and head off home. I'll call you tomorrow, though, and see how she is." He gave me a kiss and then got back behind the wheel.

I watched them disappear round the corner and headed back inside. I didn't realise just how much trouble doing a favour could cause.

Chapter 3

ALMOST two hours later, just as I was getting a bit anxious about the time, the waiter finally cleared our plates away and we asked for the bill. Sara and Amelia sorted out the maths side of things, and we all put a ten pound note into the middle. It was close enough, by the time we'd factored in all of the drinks.

We emerged onto the street, slightly the worse for wear, feeling the chill and drizzle of the late November evening.

"What now?" asked Amelia. "Club? Or last orders and reggae at the bar?"

"Either. Lead the way," said Allen.

"Not for me," I said. "It's almost half ten already. I've got a busy day tomorrow. Essays to write. I'm heading back."

Sara and Meirion looked at each other, then Sara spoke.

"We'll come with you," she said, turning to me. "Let's get a cab. We need to check in on Sophie."

That reminded me.

"Actually, do you mind if we go via the Poly on the way? She asked me to pick some books up."

"Of course, least we can do."

It was a short walk from the restaurant to our Polytechnic building, near Oxford Circus. Sara and Meirion said they'd shelter outside while I tried to sweet-talk Sam, the night security man, into letting me in. It was actually easier than I anticipated, although the pay-off was ten minutes of small talk. I think he was glad of the company.

Once I finally managed to extract myself, I walked through the deserted corridors to the lockers. It was spooky at night. It's such a lively place during the day, but at night, with dim lighting and virtually complete silence, I couldn't wait to get out.

I stopped off briefly at the toilets. Lots of wine was taking its toll. I splashed my face with water to try to wake myself up, then found Sophie's locker. As she'd mentioned, there were two bags inside. One contained clothes, which I took to be gym kit. The other was a small, empty rucksack. I loaded all of the books and files into it, headed back to reception, said goodnight to Sam and caught up with the others outside.

"Sorry about that," I said.

"What kept you?" asked Sara, flicking a cigarette away. Her breath was catching in the cold night air.

"I couldn't get away from reception. Anyway, it's all done." I indicated the bag.

We walked down to Oxford Street. It didn't take long before we saw a taxi with a yellow light. Sara hailed it, and within ten minutes we were pulling up outside the hall. As we emerged from the lift on our floor, the other two said they'd go to make coffee in the communal kitchen. Sophie's door was still slightly ajar, so I tapped before edging it open. She was in bed, but not looking very well at all.

"Brilliant, thank you so much," she said when I showed her the bag. I put it on her desk in front of the window.

"How are you feeling?"

"Not good. I've thrown up twice. You should get off before you catch the bug."

"If you're sure. Give me a knock if you need anything."

I said goodnight, and pulled her door closed, then poked my head into the kitchen and said goodnight to the others.

"I'm heading to bed," I said. "I'm knackered. Thanks for inviting me. It was a great night."

I gave them a quick update on Sophie and then returned to my room, unlocked the door and got ready for bed. I didn't see anyone else until morning. It was the last night before my world fell apart.

Chapter 4

Tuesday, November 21st, 1989

I WAS still half-asleep when the police came to see me. When they mentioned the theft from the Polytechnic equipment store, I assumed they were consulting me as a possible witness, but by the time they dragged me down to Holborn police station I was under no illusion that I was anything but the prime - in fact the only - suspect.

None of it made sense, but I couldn't explain why two horrendously-expensive Hasselblad cameras were hidden in my room. Sam maintained I'd been the only visitor that night, and no, he hadn't checked the bag he'd seen me leave with. I called for Sara and Meirion to back me up, but they just said I'd been in there longer than they'd thought I'd need, if I was just visiting a locker. Sophie confirmed that I'd dropped the rucksack off with her, but couldn't say for certain that I hadn't been back to my room first. And that all made the situation worse.

By the time I'd been interviewed under caution and warned that they were investigating a list of other potential crimes, all of which bore similar hallmarks, I was almost ready to sign a confession. It was surreal. Even if I could protest that somebody else must have got into the Polytechnic unnoticed, I couldn't explain away the physical evidence in the bottom of my wardrobe.

I half-expected to be locked in a cell immediately, but thankfully they let me go. I was left under no illusion that it would be unwise to stray too far, and that official charges would inevitably follow. I wasn't perceived as a danger to society, but equally, once they'd compiled the rest of the necessary evidence, they'd be back. And by then there'd be no escape.

I couldn't face going home. I felt confused and scared and overwhelmed with thoughts and theories that didn't stack up. So I headed to the subsidised Student Union bar in a basement in Bolsover Street to lose myself in loud music and cheap alcohol. It was still early, so relatively empty, although an indie disco was building in volume. The place would be rocking later.

I was sitting at the bar, trying to ignore a Stone Roses record and wondering if my second Martini and lemonade was such a good idea on an empty stomach, when I noticed him standing beside me.

"Hi," he said. I just groaned. The last thing I needed was somebody hitting on me, even if he did have the look of a floppy-fringed rock star.

I took a sip of my drink and then turned towards him.

"Not a good time," I said. But he didn't leave.

"Are you okay?"

I just laughed.

"Look, I'm sorry. I'll leave you alone," he said.

"If you don't mind." But still he didn't go.

"Obviously I've got to get a drink in first. What's up?" he asked. "Bad day?"

"That's one way of putting it." I looked at him properly for the first time. He seemed a nice guy, and I liked his soft northern accent. It wasn't his fault that I wasn't in the mood. The barmaid came, and he ordered a can of Red Stripe, on promotion. When the drink arrived he looked like he was going to leave, but instead he spoke again.

"I'm Danny. If you need a shoulder to cry on, or just someone to shout at, I'll be in the corner."

"Thank you," I said. "I'll bear it in mind."

"And you are?"

"Me? I'm... Well, completely fucked, if you really want to know."

"I meant your name."

"I know. God. I'm sorry. It's Anna. But yes, a very bad day so not really interested in being chatted up if it's all the same to you."

He smiled.

"I'm not chatting you up," he said. "I've got a girlfriend." There was something in the way he said it that conveyed a joyful innocence.

"So what, then?"

"Nothing really. I've just seen you here off and on, and you always seem like you're in the middle of things. But today you're on your own so I thought I'd say hello. I'm sorry if it's a bad time."

I downed my drink in one. I hoped things would start feeling better soon.

"If you want to make yourself useful, see if you can work your magic and get the barmaid back," I said. He nodded.

"What are you drinking?" he asked.

"I'm not asking you to get me a drink."

"I know, but I'd like to, if you'd let me."

I shrugged. I knew I should show gratitude, but fear had taken hold of my manners.

"Go on then," I said. "Martini and lemonade."

"Double?"

"At a minimum."

"Shit, you are having a bad day."

When the drink was poured, he passed it to me.

"So?" he said.

"So what?"

"So are you going to tell me what's the matter? I may be able to help."

"Oh, I very much doubt that."

"Try me."

I took a deep breath.

"Do you want me to summarise?"

"Go on then."

I didn't know quite where to start. I thought for a moment. There was something nice about talking to a stranger. My so-called friends hadn't exactly backed me up.

"Okay, well, I've been arrested. I'm going to get thrown off my course and I expect I'm going to end up in prison."

"Wow, that's good going. What on earth have you done?"

"What have I done? Fuck all. That's the point."

"Sorry, that doesn't make sense."

"Exactly."

He was frowning.

"Are you being serious?" he asked eventually.

"I wish I wasn't."

"Shit."

There was an awkward silence. Surely I'd done enough to scare him off.

"Should we get a table?" he said. He picked up my drink, and I had no option but to follow.

The music wasn't quite as loud in the corner, so I explained everything. Danny listened. He was very good at that.

"So, that's basically it," I said when I finished.

"But you didn't actually do it," he said.

"I know that, but try telling anyone. All the evidence suggests

I did. You can't argue with the evidence."

"How did the police know to search your room?"

I sighed.

"The bloke who runs the storeroom, Anish, reported the theft when he got to work. Sam the security guard confirmed I was the only person with access to the building."

"And you're sure the cameras weren't already in the bag when you picked it up?"

"Positive. The bag was empty. I put the books in myself. But it doesn't matter. The point is how they ended up in my wardrobe."

"Could somebody have got into your room while you were at the restaurant?"

"Possibly, but not without a key, and I had the only one with me. There was no sign of a break-in."

"I'm baffled then."

"I know. Me too. It would be fascinating if it wasn't so bloody serious. My entire future's at stake over this."

"Stay there. I'll get us another drink."

He left to go to the bar. I half expected him to make a run for it altogether. Thankfully he didn't, and he was back within a few minutes.

"So what now?" he asked, when he was seated.

"I think getting pissed is top of the agenda. And then, who knows? I'm never going to make anyone believe me."

He shrugged.

"I believe you," he said.

I laughed again. The alcohol was working its magic. "Why, though?"

"Because I trust you."

"You *trust* me? Are you mad? You don't even know me."

He rubbed his chin in a thoughtful manner. I assumed it was done ironically.

"Fair point. But, oh, I don't know. I kind of feel like I do."

"You've only just met me."

His face softened.

"Arguably, but I've noticed you. Don't take this the wrong way, but I've seen you in here. I always admired you. You're usually in a big group but you always seem like the coolest person in here. We did once stand next to each other at a Michelle Shocked gig."

"When was that?"

"Last year. Actually, not technically next to each other. You were behind me. I felt sorry for you because it didn't look like you could see much, so I let you stand in front."

"Yes! Was that you? I remember that."

"Well there you go then." He laughed. "Anyway, for what it's worth, *I* trust you."

"It's lovely that somebody does, but I still think you're mad, and it still doesn't change anything."

Before he had a chance to say anything else, I saw Todd come into the bar, looking around. I stood up without any real semblance of balance, and waved. He saw me and headed over. If I was expecting a supportive hug, I was about to be disappointed.

"I thought you were working tonight," I said, reaching out towards him.

"I am," he said, "but I'm going to be late now. I thought I'd find you here. What the fuck have you done?" Then he noticed my companion. "And more to the point, who the fuck is this?"

"I haven't done anything, and this is Danny. Danny, meet Todd, my boyfriend."

Danny stood up and offered a handshake but Todd ignored him.

"That's not what I've heard. Jesus, Anna. Stealing from your own fucking department. How stupid can you be?"

"I haven't stolen anything. I'm innocent!"

"Right. And you're pissed."

"A bit tipsy, but come on, you've got to believe me."

"I don't know what to believe. Especially when I find you in the corner with some bastard the minute my back's turned. I'm not discussing this in front of him. Outside. Now."

I turned to Danny and apologised, mortified.

"Back in a moment," I said, then turned and unsteadily followed Todd up the stairs and out onto the street outside. I wasn't in the mood for this.

Chapter 5

TO say we had a row would be an understatement. I don't like arguments at the best of times, but I wasn't going to stand in silence, getting rained on, when the one person who should have been the most supportive started shouting at me instead. Eventually, after providing improvised real-life street theatre for a couple of pedestrians, Todd stormed off, and I went back down to the basement to apologise again to Danny.

To my utter dismay, he was no longer there. The bar had been steadily filling up and getting noisier. Two girls were now at our table, and Danny was nowhere to be seen.

I swore to myself, aware that the room was spinning, feeling increasingly desperate, and ever more alone in the world. I didn't know what to do. Have another drink or just go home and cry myself to sleep? I was deciding to be sensible and choose the latter when I saw him, walking towards me.

"Sorry about that," he said. "Two cans. I couldn't hold it in any longer." That, at least, made me smile. "So that was Todd. How did it go?"

"Christ, don't ask. Listen, do you want to go somewhere else?"

"Yeah, if you like. What time do you have to get back?"

I thought for a moment.

"That's a good point, actually. I should be heading back soon. Maybe one more somewhere quieter, though?"

"How far away do you live? Don't worry, before you start. I'm not inviting myself in, but I'd head back with you. I'd just like to know you got there safely. You've had enough go wrong already."

I was momentarily taken aback by the thoughtfulness, but as the idea sank in, it seemed ever more appealing.

"It's about half an hour's walk. Only if you're sure, though. It's raining a bit. If we see a good pub we can stop on the way. Although I think I'll switch to Britvic 55s"

"Good plan," said Danny. He led the way upstairs and then to the door, holding it open for me to pass.

Thankfully, there was no sign of Todd outside on Bolsover Street, and I made sure we took a route that didn't go anywhere near the bar where he worked. I was pleased, as well, that the rain had eased to a light drizzle. It was still cold though.

As we walked, I gave Danny a summary of the confrontation. He was taller than me - who isn't? - but it felt good walking alongside him. Less of a mismatch than my boyfriend, and hence less of the irrational urge to raise my voice to ensure it carried all the way up to his ears.

As we relaxed in each other's company, we started chatting about our respective backgrounds. I mentioned growing up just outside Manchester, and how London had been such a culture shock - especially when everyone on my course seemed older and much more experienced. I told him about a freelance commission I'd undertaken, photographing bowls of fruit for a supermarket, and how I'd recently started spending my spare time helping out at a commercial studio, run by the fashion photographer Mark Colby.

In return, Danny told me about how he'd grown up in Sunderland and was inspired to follow a career in journalism when he saw a news item on TV.

"I saw this woman being interviewed, and my first thought was wow, she's gorgeous," he said.

I raised my eyebrows.

"Then I recognised a slight Sunderland accent, so I really started paying attention. And then as I listened more and heard what she was actually saying, it was like I had a revelation. She just seemed so switched on. So clever. I was hooked. I realised I wanted to meet her."

"Danny, can I break something to you? You cannot go around stalking people you see on TV."

"Haha, no, it's not like that. She's a journalist. She'd uncovered some massive fraud, and... Well, I don't know, really. It just seemed like I wished there were more people like that in the world. She became a kind of role model."

"Who was she?"

"Clare Woodbrook from the Daily Echo."

"Never heard of her, sorry. Is she aware of your devotion?"

He laughed.

"No, I expect she's blissfully ignorant. And in any case, it's really not like that. I've followed her career though. She's just brilliant. She keeps investigating major scandals and exposing them, and she's absolutely fearless. I aspire to be a tenth as good. If I can do that, I'm happy."

"Maybe she'll be writing about me, when I get sent to prison."

Danny stopped walking.

"Anna, you're not going to prison. You haven't done anything."

"That doesn't mean I'm not going, though. No jury's going to look at all that evidence and decide to believe me. I know I wouldn't if it was the other way round."

"So, we find out the truth then and give them that."

I shook my head.

"I'm not wanting to sound defeatist, but how do we do that? There's no logical explanation for any of it except the one the police have already decided on."

We started walking again. I could see my breath in the air.

"Let me help you," he said. "Let me investigate. I'll find out what really happened."

"You don't want to be taking on my problems. Honestly, you should be keeping as far away from me as possible, for your own sake."

"Anna?"

"What?"

"Can you just do me a favour?"

"What?

"Say 'okay' now, and then wait till I've said something else, and then say 'yes'?"

I tried to work that out. The effects of the drink didn't help.

"Okay," I said.

"Will you let me help you?"

"Yes."

"Perfect."

"That's not fair. You tricked me." I couldn't help smiling, despite everything.

"I can't promise it's going to work, but if you didn't do it, which you didn't, then we also know somebody else did. Whoever it was has been clever, but they're not as clever as us. Agreed?"

"If you insist."

"I do. We've just got to prove it."

We reached the entrance to my hall of residence. I asked Danny in for a cup of tea but he declined.

"Then you would think there were false pretenses," he said. "Let's meet tomorrow morning and decide on a plan of action."

He assured me he wasn't missing anything important on his course. Lots of the students would be on the march anyway. We swapped phone numbers and shook hands. It was our first-ever physical contact. As I watched him cross the road in the direction of the Baker Street tube station I hoped it wouldn't be the last. It was such a shame about his girlfriend. I'd definitely need to find out more about her.

Four other people were waiting by the lift when I arrived. I saw one nudge another, who cast a glance in my direction, before all four then looked away. The journey to the eighth floor passed in a desperately slow silence. I got out. The others were all going to a higher floor. As the doors closed, I suddenly heard excited voices before they were all whisked out of earshot.

Rather than go straight to my room, I decided to drop in on the common room to speak to as many of my housemates as possible, to explain what had happened, and see if they had any bright ideas. Normally at least a handful of them would be in there, watching Amelia's portable TV. The lights were off. I flicked the switch but there was nobody there, just a rectangle in the dust where the TV should have been.

It all seemed so strange. These were supposed to be my friends. Where were they? Why were they not supporting me? I decided to check in on Sophie to see how she was feeling, but there was no answer when I knocked on her door. I moved to Amelia's room and tried there instead. I thought I could hear voices, but when I knocked they stopped. I called out and tried again, but nobody came to the door.

I gave up and returned to my room. It was small and cold and horribly lonely. From the window I could see cars streaming along Marylebone Road. It was a long way down. I wondered how long it would take me to fall, and how blissfully carefree the journey would be, until I landed and all my problems simply vanished along with my heartbeat. I shuddered. I wasn't quite there yet.

I just didn't know what to do. My only friend in the whole world seemed to be some bloke that I'd just met in a bar. And how was I to know that I could trust him, really? Maybe his sudden appearance wasn't quite such a coincidence after all. Maybe he was part of this unknown, twisted conspiracy against me. Maybe right now he was laughing with his cohorts, describing my abject misery, while raising a glass to a job well done. As Joseph Heller said in Catch-22, just because you're paranoid doesn't mean they're not after you. Somebody had definitely decided I was expendable, but I didn't know who or why.

"Right, you bastards," I said to myself. "I'm going to fucking show the lot of you."

Chapter 6

Wednesday, November 22nd, 1989

THE situation didn't look any better the following morning. I had a terrible night, sleeping fitfully, so when I finally decided to get up and face the day I was overcome by an overwhelming tiredness.

In the kitchen I took a tea bag from the box in my cupboard, but when I went to get milk from the fridge I noticed that everything had been labelled with the name of its owner. Somebody had stuck a sign on the wall warning of the dire consequences of using something that wasn't your own. Until this moment, we'd operated a trust system, but it seemed like those days were over. Charming, I thought. Well you can all just fuck off.

I tried to clear my head of the growing sense of neurosis, but it felt like a losing battle. I was supposed to be meeting Danny in the cafe at ten. Was it just so he could continue to laugh at me? And yet, deep down, I knew I was being irrational. He'd offered to help. God knows I needed someone. If he was part of the problem then so be it. It was a risk I was going to have to take.

I had a shower but couldn't be bothered to sort out my hair, so decided on a hat, teamed with my big duffel coat and a scarf to keep out the worst of the wind. He was already seated at a table when I arrived, wearing jeans and an ice blue sweatshirt, his leather jacket over the back of his chair. He smiled when he saw me walking towards him. Immediately I felt better. And then the smile turned into a laugh.

"What's funny?" I asked, feeling the limit of my patience fast approaching.

"Nothing, it's just..." His grin was getting wider.

"What?"

"I'm sorry. Don't take this the wrong way, but you look a bit like Paddington, that's all."

I looked down at my outfit. And then I saw the funny side.

"And who are you? Hercule Poirot?" I said, giving in to an involuntary smile. "You need to work on the moustache."

He stood up and we embraced, and suddenly I felt a whole lot better again.

I removed the coat and scarf, but the hat had to stay for reasons of vanity. The cafe was warm and busy, with steamed up windows and the aroma of bacon. The tables had seen better days, but the other customers didn't seem to mind.

We ordered a pot of tea and two full English breakfasts. I hadn't even given a thought to food the previous day, but my appetite was fast returning. When the food arrived, I poured the tea and then we both tucked in. Once we'd finished and the plates were taken, I returned to the pot and poured us each a second cup.

"So," he said, confronting the unspoken conundrum. "Any news?"

"Since last night? Nothing really, except my housemates all seem to hate me." I explained about the missing TV, the food labels and the way everyone seemed to be avoiding me.

"Do you think any of them know what's going on?"

"I don't think so. I was out with four of them." I raised my hand to cover a yawn. "Sorry, I didn't sleep too well. The others on my floor are a lad from Iran, I think, called Bahrom. We never see him. He's got his own group of friends, and stays away a lot so he's there maybe once a fortnight. Then there are the two Jasons: Jason Ashburn and Jason Critchlow. Jason Ashburn is a bit of a geek, nice lad but seems completely harmless. He's only interested in work so never really socialises, although we think he fancies Sophie. He's out of his depth though. She'd eat him. And the other Jason is away, I think. He's on a placement somewhere. We haven't seen him in weeks."

"Have you ever fallen out with any of them?"

"Me? No, not really. We have the occasional disagreement, as you do when you live with people, but I'm the most laid-back person I know. I just want to take pictures and be good at it. I tend to get on with everyone."

"Okay. So we agree it's unlikely it's some sort of vendetta?"

"I hope not, anyway. I can't see it."

"So talk me through Monday night again. Everything you can remember, just in case you missed anything last night."

I went through it all from the start, from Amelia's invitation, to arriving home, via the Polytechnic. I mentioned how Sophie had been taken ill and Todd had given her a lift home. That seemed to spark something in Danny.

"I hate to say this, but Todd?" he said.

"What about him?"

"I've only met him very briefly but he didn't seem... how can I say it politely? He didn't seem particularly friendly."

"No, I was a bit shocked by that."

"Have you known him long?"

"A few months."

"And you trust him?"

"Yeah, of course."

The waitress returned and asked if we wanted anything else. I think she was keen for us to vacate the table. Danny asked her to give us a few minutes.

"You don't think he could have let himself into your room while he knew you were out?" he continued, once she'd left.

"No, it's impossible. Why would he do that? He doesn't have a key. And before you ask, no, he can't have secretly copied it either. It's always on me."

"You're sure?"

"Completely."

"And he's done nothing to make you doubt him? Never been angry with you before?"

"No, it's all been good, generally. Just the odd moment. He was a bit moody at the weekend, and I think he was annoyed I wasn't going home with him after the restaurant, which is probably why he said he wasn't coming back. Aside from that, and then yesterday, he's normally been okay."

"Just okay?"

"Better than okay. It's been good."

Danny nodded.

"Right," he said after a moment. "This is difficult. There's nothing that obviously stands out. And yet, there must be."

"Because?"

"Because you didn't do it."

"As long as you still believe me."

"I still believe you."

He placed his hand on mine. I perceived it as comforting rather than an attempt to seduce me. I saw the waitress giving us a dirty look.

"I'll tell you what I'll do," Danny continued, letting go. "I'll go to the hall of residence now. I think all lectures are cancelled because of the march, so hopefully there'll be a few of the others there. I'll ask around, see what I can find out, and get a sense of the place."

"Are you sure? It's a bit like the lion's den at the moment."

"It's the best place to start."

"You're brave. But thank you."

"What are you up to?"

"I'm going to go and see Todd and see if I can smooth things out with him, and have a proper conversation."

"Good luck. Call me when you get back, or I'll call you."

"Perfect."

I tried to pour a third cup of tea, but the pot was empty. We decided to leave it there, so I followed Danny to the counter. We split the bill.

"One thing that's bothering me," I said, as we headed to the door. "You said you've got a girlfriend. Is she going to be happy with you helping a damsel in distress?"

Danny smiled.

"I don't know. I haven't really thought about it."

"What's her name? Do you live with her?"

"She's called Shelley."

"Ooh, like the poet?"

"Something like that. And no, I don't live with her. She's from back home, although we have weekends when we can."

"Nice. And, does, er, Shelley write you romantic poems as the name implies? During periods of prolonged absence?"

He started to blush.

"No."

"Haha. She clearly does. And I bet you write them back. Roses are red, violets are blue, I love you Shelley and you love me too."

"No!"

"Fibber. You're going red."

"I'm very hot."

I started to laugh.

"Well, I'll tell you what. I won't mention it again, on one condition."

"What's that?"

"That you never again say I look like Paddington."

Chapter 7

DANNY took a small bunch of flowers and a large box of chocolates to the checkout of the twenty-four-hour convenience store on Baker Street, and winced when he was told the price. It was a necessary investment, though. He tried to avoid eye contact with the houseman as he walked past reception of the hall of residence and then took the lift to the eighth floor, thankful that nobody else had got in with him. When the doors opened, he paused for a moment, took a breath of air filled with the scent of burnt toast and stale cigarettes, and decided he could do this. It was time to embrace the role.

Anna had explained the layout: two rows of four rooms, on opposite sides of the building, with a communal kitchen and common room in between. One side was boys, one was girls. He turned right, looking for room 804, but when it wasn't there he entered the common room to cross to the other side. Two girls were deep in conversation. He tried to make out their words, looking for any indication of the prevailing mood, but they stopped and looked up when they noticed him.

"Can I help you?" asked the one nearest the window. She had dark hair and dark eyes, and was smoking a roll-up cigarette.

"Sorry, I'm just looking for a room," he said.

"Are they for me?" asked the other, looking at the flowers. Her bright red hair was striking.

Danny smiled and blushed. So far so good.

"No, I, er..." he began.

"Leave him alone," said the first.

Danny walked through the common room, out the other side, and then found 804 at the end of the row. He knocked, loud enough that he knew they'd hear.

After a moment he returned to the common room.

"Hi again," he said. "Sorry to interrupt. I wonder if you could help, actually? I was looking for Anna. Do you know if she's due back?"

"Anna? Ha. Good luck there," said the first girl. "Who are you?"

"Danny. Just a friend."

"And you want Anna? Just a friend and you're carrying flowers?"

Danny looked down and blushed again.

"Kind of a new friend." He moved the flowers and chocolates behind his back.

"Does Todd know you're here?"

"Who's Todd?"

"Anna's boyfriend."

Danny paused.

"What? Seriously? As in...?"

She nodded.

"Looks like she's done you as well," she said. "Lucky escape. I'm Sara, by the way. This is Sophie."

"Hi Sara, pleased to meet you. And Sophie."

He let out a deep breath.

"But she said..."

"You can't trust a word she says. Sorry to break the news."

"Do you mind?" Danny indicated to a chair.

"Feel free."

He undid his jacket and then sat down, placing the flowers and chocolates on the table.

"Are you sure they're still together?"

"As far as I know," said Sophie.

"God, I must look a complete twat." He started removing the cellophane from the Milk Tray. "I don't suppose I'm leaving these then. Fancy a chocolate?"

"Rude not to." Sara reached out for the box. "Thank you."

"Just one then I'll leave you to it," said Sophie. She stood up. "Catch you later, Sara, if you're around?"

"I'll be back after the march, whenever that is," she said.

Sophie turned and walked out of the room.

"Sorry to sound stupid," Danny continued, once he was alone with Sara, "but what do you mean you can't trust a word Anna says? Aside from the obvious. She seemed so nice."

"You haven't heard, then?" She started rolling another cigarette, licking the edge of the Rizla paper.

"Haven't heard what?"

"She's been thieving from the Poly."

"What, Anna has? Are we talking about the same Anna?"

"It was a shock to us as well. But yeah, apparently."

"Jesus. What did she pinch?"

"A couple of cameras. We had the police here and everything."

"When was this?"

"The police were here yesterday. She pinched them Monday night."

"Wow." Danny shook his head and took a moment to examine his surroundings. There were a few film posters on the walls. The furniture was worn, but reasonably clean if you ignored the stains on the carpets. "So what happened?"

"Just that. They turned up, searched her room, found the stuff and nicked her. Stupid bitch." Sara laughed. Danny thought he detected malice in her voice. She seemed to be enjoying the scandal.

"Jesus." He took another chocolate, then offered the box. "Help yourself. "I don't know what to say. Are they sure it was her?"

"Yeah, of course."

"Has she pinched anything else?"

"That's what we were just discussing. We've had all sorts go missing here. Just little stuff like food and that, but it makes you wonder."

"Has she been splashing the cash about?"

"No. I'll give her that. We're all skint. You know what it's like if you're a student. Maybe she's hoarding it though. We've no idea what she's up to."

The door opened, and a young man walked in, carrying a briefcase.

"Hiya Jase," said Sara. "You all right?"

"Yeah, lectures are cancelled so I'm cracking on here. Sophie around?"

"Just gone to her room. Fancy a chocolate? You don't mind, do you?" she added, turning to Danny.

"No, help yourself. Hi, I'm Danny," he said to the new arrival. "I was just getting told about Anna."

"Jason. God yeah, that was a shock. You can never tell though, can you?" He took a chocolate from the box but remained standing.

"Do you think it was definitely her? Nobody else could have left the stuff in there?"

Jason shrugged.

"I was in here all night watching TV," he said. "The girls were at the restaurant. Nobody went near the rooms till Sophie came back, but she went straight to hers apart from when I heard her in the bathroom. She had a guy with her, Anna's boyfriend actually, but he just dropped her off and went. He didn't go anywhere near Anna's."

"Definitely nobody's been near her room since Monday," added Sara, taking over. "I mean, we've always been fairly laid-back with locking doors and that, but nobody's got anything worth nicking. We're a bit more careful now, mind."

"I don't blame you."

"Oh, and she had a bag. Me and Meirion waited outside the Poly for her then we all got a taxi back. She was in there ages. She was just supposed to be going to a locker."

"Did you tell the police that?"

"Of course. I mean, I didn't want to cause her trouble but... And actually, you know what else? Her face looked damp, now I think about it, as though she was sweating."

Danny stood up.

"Well, I don't suppose there's much point hanging around. Tell her I came if you see her, for what it's worth."

"I doubt we'll see her," said Jason. "Shall do though, if we do."

"I'll leave you the flowers and chocolates. Seems like the least I can do. Maybe see you in the bar sometime?"

"I'll look out for you," said Sara, lighting the cigarette. "And better luck next time."

"Aye, fingers crossed."

Danny said goodbye and headed back to the lift. Mission accomplished.

Chapter 8

I THOUGHT about phoning Todd to make sure he was in, but I didn't want to take the risk that he'd refuse to see me, or worse still, decline to answer the call. No doubt he'd be home, though, given the state of inertia caused by the imminent march. He was supposed to be at work that evening, but hopefully he hadn't also taken the lunchtime shift.

I took the bus to Swiss Cottage, and sat at the front, being shaken by the rattles of the diesel engine, looking out of the window, pondering life. The north London traffic was heavy. There were so many people, so many cars, with headlights already on in the gloom. Who were they? Where were they all going? Why did they all look to have such a sense of purpose and direction when my own life was falling apart? What reward would I have for working so hard, now everything I'd striven for was so close to collapse?

It was a short walk from the bus stop to Todd's flat. We'd done it many times, in the first flush of early romance, holding hands, or chasing each other, just generally fooling around and happy to be alive. Not today.

I pressed the bell, then waited. Nothing. I pressed it again.

Again nothing. Then after a full half-minute or more, I thought I heard movement inside. I pressed the bell for a third time. Through the textured glass panel I could see a figure, no clearer than a shadow, and it was coming towards me.

Todd opened the door. He's never been the sharpest of dressers, but he looked particularly scruffy, unshaven, and maybe sleep-deprived. I could relate to that last bit.

"Hi," I said. He just looked at me, as though I was a stranger. "Can I come in?"

He opened the door wider and stepped aside. I walked past, not really knowing which way to go: right for the living room or straight on for the kitchen? The bedroom was upstairs. I didn't think we'd be going there. I stopped, waiting for him to lead the way. Living room it was. It also didn't look like I was going to be offered a cup of tea.

"What are you doing here?" he asked at last, when I'd taken a place on the sofa. I hoped he was going to join me, but he stayed standing. It was not a good sign, and put me at an even greater physical disadvantage. He really did look very tall.

"I just want to talk to you," I said. "Explain things. Make sure we're okay."

"I'm not sure there's anything more to say."

"What do you mean? Of course there is. I hate falling out with you. I hate falling out with anyone, but you especially."

"Anna." He sighed, then stopped, looking beyond me. "I don't know what you want me to do."

"I don't want you to *do* anything. Maybe just listen to me. Be there for me. Try to help me work out what the fuck is going on."

"You make me laugh."

"*What?*"

"What do you mean 'what'?"

"For fuck's sake. It's a simple enough question. What do you mean I make you laugh? I've come here to see you because I'm scared, Todd. Scared of losing you, scared of all the trouble that seems to be landing on me like a fucking tidal wave. Not for your bloody amusement."

"Yeah, well, you should have thought about that before nicking the gear."

"*What?*"

"Oh, here we go again."

"Todd! You of all people. I did *not* steal anything. Surely you believe that."

"I don't know how you can sit there and say that."

"I can sit here and say it because it's true."

"Not according to the police."

"Jesus."

I was momentarily lost for words. This couldn't be happening.

"So you're saying you believe them rather than me?"

"The evidence was there, Anna. I mean, how well do I really know you? I thought I knew you. I thought we were fine. Then I find out you're a thief and you're seeing somebody behind my back. I think you've got problems, I really do."

"Right." I stood up. I really felt like hitting something. Ideally a bottle. "Well, you know what? I'm not a thief, I'm not seeing anybody."

"And you expect me to believe that?"

"Oh, you know what? Believe what the fuck you like. I'm going. I don't need this." I headed to the door. "And in the meantime, thanks for the support. But now you can just *piss off.*"

I walked out and slammed the door shut behind me. Not, perhaps, my most eloquent put down. I felt hollow inside. Clearly that hadn't gone as well as I'd hoped, but I was about to find out that things could get worse again.

Chapter 9

AT times of great stress I occasionally do weird things. In arguments I tend to fix on examining some detail in the room, counting the number of times the wallpaper pattern repeats or how many floor tiles are in each row. It helps me dehumanise the situation, I think. I've always tended to focus trauma onto abstract material things. As I walked across the courtyard, back to the entrance to my tower block, I started counting paving slabs, as though some magic number would be the combination for the lock that was closing ever more tightly on my brain. I didn't attempt to avoid standing on the cracks, though. I'm not mad.

The houseman, Billy, stopped me as I walked through the door to reception. I was expecting to be told that I'd now been evicted on top of everything else, but instead he passed me an envelope, with my name written by hand on the outside.

"Chin up," he said as I thanked him. I don't know how much he knew, but I liked Billy. He always seemed friendly and non-judgemental, which is handy when rowdy students are turning up at all hours, in various states of inebriation, with guests in tow for late-night activities of dubious morality. That was my experience, anyway, although maybe he just thought I was a lost cause.

I opened the envelope when I got into the lift. It was a note from Danny.

Hi Anna,

I hope all went well with Todd. Fingers crossed.

I made some enquiries and met Sara, Sophie and one of the Jasons. They're pretty sure it's you, but we know the truth. We'll show them.

Keep the faith, no matter how hard this seems. We make a good team I think. Call me when you get a chance. Let's meet this evening if you're free.

I'm thinking of you.

Danny

x

Inside, a part of me melted. If Danny was genuine, I didn't understand why he was being so nice to me. For the first time since this whole thing started, I felt anger and confusion giving way to tears. I didn't know what I'd done to deserve support from a stranger, when those closest to me were making every effort to distance themselves, but it was something to cling to. I left the lift, went straight to my room, and the tears began to flow in earnest.

It took half an hour before I felt up to facing the world. I retouched my make-up to hide the worst, then looked for my phonecard so I could call Danny from one of the phones in the lobby. I found the card, but just as an extra dent to my resilience, remembered I'd already used the last of the credit. Why was everything so hard?

I either had to go back out, in the cold, and walk round to the corner shop to spend money I didn't have, or I had to see if any of my lovely housemates would lend me a card for a quick call. The thought of walking into the common room and confronting them filled me with dread, and something approximating shame. But what did I have to feel shameful about? I'd done nothing wrong. I opened the common room door.

Five of them were in there, freshly back from protesting, or just taking the afternoon off. All except Bahrom and the other Jason. Conversation stopped. Jason Ashburn looked at me. The others all looked away.

"All right, guys?" I said. I hate the word 'guys' normally, but I hoped it would bring a certain lightness to proceedings. Nobody spoke.

"Jesus. You do know I'm innocent, don't you? You do know I'm being stitched up?"

Still all five stayed silent. Meirion turned towards the window, while Sophie reached for a mug and seemed to take an eternity staring at it, as though deciding whether or not to take a sip.

"So we're not speaking then. Brilliant. And I don't suppose anyone would care to lend me a phonecard?"

"Sorry, Anna, I haven't got one," said Jason. He may even have been telling the truth. Sophie continued looking at the mug.

"I'll take that as a no, then," I said at last. "And yes, Sophie, I did piss in it. So fuck the lot of you."

I returned to my room, grabbed my leather jacket, then locked my door behind me as I headed to the shop.

On second thoughts, calling from the lobby probably wasn't wise anyway, as I didn't know who would be listening. I had to assume my enemy, whoever it was, was close enough to want to hurt me and that meant it could be anyone. I bought a phonecard from the nearest newsagent, then headed along Baker Street until I saw a callbox. Danny answered on the third ring.

"How was Todd?" he asked.

"It's finished. Next question?"

"Shit, I'm sorry. What happened?"

"Oh Danny, you don't even want to know. He's a twat. Does that sum it up?"

"Fair play."

"How did you get on?"

He gave me a swift recap of his visit, and told me about the box of chocolates. Even if this investigation came to nothing, I decided, he'd go far.

"So what next?" I asked when he'd finished. "I'm running out of ideas here. And phone credit."

"We need to meet again, if you're free. What time is it now?"

"Just gone half past five."

"Should we say half six? Bolsover Street? We can always move on if it's too crowded. There's a river cruise thing on tonight so it should be quiet."

"Perfect. I'll see you there. And thanks, Danny. You don't know how much this means."

I got back in the lift at the hall, but as the doors were closing someone stuck his arm in the way. The doors opened again and he stepped in to join me. I felt him looking me up and down.

"You're Anna?" he asked once the doors had closed.

"Yup," I said, not in the mood for conversation.

"You're quite the celebrity."

"God." I took a step to the right. He was standing too close. "It's not intentional."

"We should get together," he said. "I've got a bit of a thing for bad girls."

Thankfully the doors opened before I had to worry about adding assault to my list of charges. I gave him a massive two fingers once the doors had safely closed and he was on his way to a higher floor.

I didn't see the point in trying to speak to anyone, so went straight to my room. There was a piece of A4 paper stuck on the door. As I got closer I could read the writing. One word. Thief. Nice touch. I snatched it off, then unlocked and opened the door before screwing it up as tightly as I could and throwing it in the direction of my overflowing bin. I missed.

I wasn't feeling hungry but decided I should try to make the effort so I boiled the kettle for a quick cup of tea and then started preparing cheese on toast. I had the kitchen to myself, which was unusual, although frankly I no longer cared. I'd had enough of their pettiness.

In my room, I was just finishing the final slice when there was another knock on the door. I was expecting it to be Jason, maybe coming to apologise, but when I opened it my heart sank yet further. It was the police.

"Ms Burgin," said the taller of the two. "We'd like you to come with us."

Chapter 10

"HAVE I got an option?" I asked.

"You can either come willingly or we can use the handcuffs," he said.

I looked at my watch. It was approaching six. I really didn't have time for this.

"Will we be long?"

"Save your questions for the station, miss." And that was the end of that. I was led away to the waiting car. Billy averted his gaze as I passed.

I was signed in and then shown through to an interview room and made to wait. I don't often regret having a cup of tea, but the last one was beginning to cause me deep discomfort. How come on TV dramas the suspects never need the toilet? It was just one more very real thing to worry about.

Time passed and my already-heightened sense of anxiety got ever more intense. Where were they? What were they going to do with me? I looked at my watch again. I was already late for

Danny. I needed them to get this over with as quickly as they could.

But they didn't. They didn't even come to see me. Seven came and went. Then seven-thirty. I pictured Danny, alone in the bar, waiting for me. Perhaps he'd be concerned at first, assuming that I was just running late. But when would concern give way to annoyance? Then frustration, then outright anger?

He'd give up on me, deciding I was just an unreliable time-waster, assuming that everything everyone said about me was true. The one person who'd offered to help me, being alienated through absolutely no fault of my own. There was no way to relay a message. My one chance to actually have somebody on my side, utterly destroyed - and for what? So I could sit on my own in an interview room, acutely in need of the toilet, feeling increasingly nauseous, desperately wanting to know what on earth was going on. Where were they?

They came just after eight. There was no apology from either of them. DS Phil Matthews made the introductions then asked me to confirm my name for the tape, while DC Gordon Kendrick sat in silence, making notes. And then they started to grill me. Where had I been on certain dates? Could anyone vouch for me? Who was I selling the stuff to? What was I doing with the money? Apparently I could expect a degree of leniency at court if I'd be willing to testify against the other members of my gang.

They left after twenty minutes, saying they'd be back in a moment. Another hour passed. Then they returned and it started again. The same questions, trying to break me. But I was broken already, and I couldn't give information that I simply didn't know.

It was nearly twenty past ten by the time they decided they'd had enough and I was allowed to leave. There was no offer of a lift home. Presumably it's perfectly safe for a young woman of waif-like stature to walk through deserted London streets on her own, late at night. Nothing could possibly go wrong there.

I caught the first bus I saw, heading in any direction, and sat back amongst the drunks and night shift workers, trying to think of a plan but devoid of any inspiration. The bus passed Centre Point on the way to Oxford Circus. At least I was going in vaguely the right direction. I got off when I saw the familiar Topshop frontage, then headed up Regent Street towards the BBC. The Student Union bar was on the far side. If I could make it there safely, I might at least find someone else heading back my way, who I could tag along behind. At least they'd hear my screams.

I made it to the bar. There was no sign of Danny. Why would there be? I was just in time to order a drink, so I made it a triple. And then I sat at the bar, with my head in my hands, the tail end of the disco pounding through my brain, wondering really what was the point of anything any more. A girl next to me was smoking so I asked if I could buy a cigarette. The alcohol on a largely empty stomach was making me terribly light-headed. The nicotine made it worse. But hey, bollocks to everything. Nothing really mattered any more. And then I felt somebody's hand on my shoulder.

"I didn't know you smoked," said Danny.

I looked at him, then at the cigarette burning between my fingers. I tried to hide it behind my back.

"I don't," I said, each syllable accompanied by a grey wisp of smoke from my mouth. The irony wasn't lost. "What are you still doing here? God, I am so sorry."

"Come on," he said. "Let's go somewhere quiet."

He offered me his hand. I looked at the cigarette again, then poked it into an overflowing ashtray on the bar, and reached out towards him. His skin was warm, his grip reassuring. My own hand felt tiny.

Danny led me back upstairs, and outside into the cold night air. The sound of the music was reduced to a low bass thump.

"I'm so pleased to see you," I said. Instinctively I gave him a hug. It felt awkward at first but he didn't seem to mind.

"What happened?" he asked when I finally released him.

"Oh, God. It was the police. More questions. The bastards made me wait for ages. I don't think they like students at the best of times."

"It's not surprising at the moment."

"How come you're still here? I thought you'd be gone hours ago."

He grinned.

"I knew you'd turn up eventually. And anyway I wanted to see you."

There was something in his voice that seemed to hide a subtext.

"Is Shelley okay with you hanging around bars waiting for other women?"

He laughed.

"I'll tell you what, I'll make you a promise."

"Go on."

"If I ever overstep the boundary, I'll let you slap me."

Despite everything, the world already seemed slightly less foreboding with Danny around.

"Luckily for you I'm not the violent type," I said.

We set off, walking back in the direction of my hall of residence. I wanted to link arms but I had to be respectful. I felt safe with him beside me, but I didn't want to embarrass either of us.

I told Danny all about my police interview. He filled me in on the full details of his conversation at the hall.

"So, pretty much they're sure you did it," he said when he'd finished.

"And yet you still believe me?"

He nodded.

"But why? Even I'm beginning to think I must have done it. Maybe I had a drink spiked with something that made me lose all recollection. I don't *think* I did, but I just don't know what else explains it."

"What was the name of the security man you spoke to?"

"Where? When I picked the books up?"

Danny nodded.

"That was Sam. That's not his real name. It's Sanjit or something. He's Indian, but he tells everyone to call him Sam."

"And he wouldn't vouch for you?"

"That's half the problem. He would for when I was chatting to him, but then he let me go off on my own. If only I'd made him come with me."

"But you didn't know you needed to do that."

"I know, but the place was giving me the creeps."

"And you definitely didn't see anyone else?"

"No. But I didn't go anywhere near the storeroom."

We turned off Marylebone High Street. My tower block came into view.

"Sara said it looked like you were sweating when you came out."

"*What?* It was freezing." That stopped me. Then I had a realisation. "Jesus. I splashed my face with water in the toilets. I was trying to sober up."

"There you go then. See? Rational explanation. There'll be one somewhere."

I wished I could share Danny's confidence.

"Would you like to come in for a cup of tea?" I asked as we approached the stairs to my building.

"It's probably best not to," he said.

"Why? In case I try to molest you?"

"Ha ha, no. Because I'd probably meet your housemates, which would kind of blow my cover."

"Oh yeah. Sorry about that."

"That's okay." He put his arm round me and gave me a squeeze. "Tell you what, should we do a deal?"

"Go on."

"Just so we know where we stand, and so it doesn't get in the way, should we just agree to be friends over this? Special friends. If you say something to me that's vaguely salacious, I'm not going to assume you're trying anything on, and likewise backwards."

"If you like."

"Don't get me wrong, I've worshipped you from afar for ages and it's a privilege to speak to you, but we've got to trust each other without worrying that either of us is, I don't know, developing an agenda."

"So I can give you a hug because I like giving hugs, and you're not going to automatically think I'm trying to compete with Shelley?"

"Something like that."

I thought for a moment.

"Sounds like a plan," I said at last. "Anyway, as we've clearly seen, I'm shit at relationships."

"You can't say that just because Todd's been a twat."

"Oh, Danny. I've had three proper boyfriends since I moved to London, if you don't count the ones that lasted twenty-four hours. Or actually less than that in most cases. And you know what? They all ended up turning into colossal knobs."

"And you don't like colossal knobs?"

"Danny!" I blushed for him. He started to laugh.

I offered him my hand. He took it and we shook.

"It will be an honour to be your friend," I said.

"And likewise."

It was the moment that sealed a special relationship. We were nearly at reception.

"I'll walk you to the lift then leave you there," he said. "As long you're sure you're going to be all right?"

"I'm pretty sure nothing else can go wrong. Are you going to be all right getting home? I don't even know where you live."

"Kentish Town. But, yeah, I'll get the tube, or a night bus."

"I'm sorry it's so late."

"Don't worry. Should we meet in the morning for coffee?"

"I'd prefer tea, but do you not have lectures?"

"Nothing I can't miss. There's hardly anyone in at the moment, with everything going on." He suggested 10am at another cafe that wasn't too far away. I agreed, then pressed the button for the lift.

"Come here," I said while we waited for it to arrive. I gave him a big hug. He stroked my hair, which I'd normally find annoying, but I really didn't mind. It was a shame about the deal, and a shame about Shelley, but I'd try to respect both of them. He was probably right. It'd simplify things. The lift arrived and we said our farewells with a peck. The last thing I saw before the doors closed was Danny smiling at me, looking brave and strong and just so reassuring. My life was falling apart but part of me felt like the luckiest girl in the world.

Danny nodded to the houseman on his way out of the building, then headed across the courtyard in the direction of the Baker Street Underground station. He didn't see the blow coming, but he felt it hard, as it connected with immense force to the back of his legs. He fell to the pavement, stunned, feeling agonising pain shooting up his body, his mind blank in shock. The bat connected a second time, narrowly missing his knees, but instead smashing into his shins, causing a new wave of white-hot pain.

He looked up, hands raised to try to protect his face. A figure was towering over him, identity concealed behind a black balaclava. A steel toecap connected with his ribs, again and again, the pressure and ferocity increasing. Danny fought for breath, then felt a fist ram hard into his stomach. As he lowered his arms, another fist punched him hard across the cheek.

The figure leaned over him.

"That's your final warning," he said. "Next time it'll be serious. Leave the bitch alone."

Chapter 11

Thursday, November 23rd, 1989

I TURNED up to the cafe early, but as I opened the door, I saw Danny had beaten me to it. He was on his own at a corner table, head half hidden behind a newspaper.

"Morning," I said as I approached, weaving my way through the other customers, and trying to sound more cheerful than I felt. He dropped the newspaper and I got the first sight of the state of him. The feigned joviality vanished. "Jesus, Danny, what happened to your face?"

He winced.

"The face got off lightly. You should see the rest of me."

"Fuck. Are you okay? Did somebody jump you?"

He nodded, eyes tensing with the effort of the movement.

"I'd give you a hug, but it's a bit painful actually standing up," he said.

"But... Jesus. When was this?"

"Last night, just after I left you."

He gave me a summary of the assault and then the warning

not to have any more to do with me. At least I assumed it was me.

"And he actually called me a bitch?"

"Yup."

"Bastard. The rest I can take, but that's going too far."

Danny smiled then gasped in pain.

"Please, don't make me laugh. It really does hurt."

"Seriously, though, have you spoken to the police?"

"Not yet, but what can they do? There's no witness. It could have been anyone. They'll say it was just a standard mugging but that could happen to anybody."

"Did he take your wallet?"

"No."

"And he specifically warned you against speaking to me?"

He nodded again.

"I'm not a detective but that's not a standard mugging. Listen, Danny, let's stop this, here and now. I can't have this. You can't have anything to do with me. We'll stay friends if you'll have me, but for heaven's sake, I never intended this, I am so sorry."

"Grab a chair," he said. I did as instructed, then he reached across to cup my hands in his. "This doesn't change anything. If anything it makes me more determined. It may not be connected but it may mean we're getting close."

"But seriously, Danny..."

"Seriously yourself. I'm not quitting now."

"But look at yourself! I'm not taking that risk, even if you are."

"Shhh."

He put a finger to my lips. I seriously thought about kissing it, but wasn't sure if that would be in breach of our pact. I took a deep breath.

"But what do we actually know?" I asked at last.

The waitress arrived. I wasn't sure the cafe was the most

hygienic, so I limited my risk to a pot of tea and two slices of toast. Danny already had tea but ordered another anyway.

"Are we any further forward?" I persevered, when we were back on our own.

"I don't know. I didn't think so, but someone's been rattled."

"Did you get a look at him?"

"Not really, his face was covered, but he was a big bloke. Six foot plus. He had a kind of Scouse accent, though."

"Oh my God." I ran my hand through my hair.

"What's up?"

"I don't want to think what I'm thinking."

"What are you thinking?"

"I'm thinking I know someone from Liverpool who's six foot two and pissed off with me. It can't be, though, surely. There must be thousands of people from Liverpool in London."

Danny looked straight at me with his crystal clear blue eyes.

"Todd?"

I nodded.

"You didn't see anything else?" I asked. "Like what he was wearing?"

"I didn't see much. It was so dark. He was wearing black and a balaclava. Actually I did notice something. He had a big ring on."

"Which finger?"

"Must have been right hand. Middle."

"God, Danny."

"Let me guess. Todd's got a ring?"

I nodded again.

"Right hand. A black onyx gothy biker thing."

"That sounds like it."

"Fuck." I needed a moment to let all this sink in. Seeing Danny in such obvious pain just made things worse. This hadn't been the work of a random mugger; it was entirely down to his association with me, for whatever reason. Maybe they should just lock me up and throw away the key. Much better for everyone. I was fighting back my emotions.

"Danny, I am so sorry." I didn't know what else to say.

"It's not your fault."

"But it is. Of course it is."

"It really isn't. You're not responsible for other people."

"I know, but..."

"Look, it may not have been him," he said. "If it was, so what? It doesn't necessarily mean he's got anything to do with the cameras."

"He was there, though. That would make sense. I don't know how he got in my room without a key, or what on earth he's playing at, but he must have done it when he was dropping Sophie off."

"No."

"What now?" I looked at Danny, full of expectation, hoping we were on the verge of a breakthrough, even if there was so much that didn't make sense.

"There's one problem with that," he said.

"Is there?"

"Quite a big one."

"God. What?"

"Even if he somehow managed to get into your room, he didn't have the stuff. That didn't get stolen till later."

"Ah." That stopped me. I leaned back in my chair, and looked up to the ceiling, then returned my elbows to the table, my head in my hands. "God, my brain hurts. Back to square one?"

"Not exactly. We should go to see him."

"*What?*"

"Both of us."

"Are you mad? I'll go, but you can't. Didn't he just beat you up and say to have no more to do with me?"

"If it was him, yes."

"And which part of that is turning up with me?"

"The part that wants to know if it was him. That part that says we're not going to be intimidated. The part that says we can look him in the eye and he can get the message that we're not going to give up. And hopefully the part that helps us work out whether he's acting out of jealousy because he's seen me with you, or if he's up to something else that we haven't worked out yet."

"Are you sure you really want to do this?"

"Never more so."

I finished my cup of tea and poured a second, offering Danny a refill, but he declined. I moved the newspaper out of the way, then reached for his hand and gave it a squeeze.

"Are you up to going anywhere? How are you feeling? Really?"

"A bit tender, but I'm okay."

"I don't know what to say, really, except thank you."

He smiled.

"It's a pleasure, honestly. I'm just happy to help. This is what I want to do. Make a difference. Talking of which..." He turned the newspaper to face me.

I wasn't sure what I was supposed to be looking at. It was a copy of this morning's Daily Echo. I'd seen it on a newsstand outside as well. The front page lead was about a pharmaceutical company using cancer research donations to pay for lavish holidays for high-ranking executives. It was a scandal, clearly, but I wasn't sure whether I was supposed to have an opinion, aside from the obvious sense of outrage.

Danny indicated the byline and then I understood.

"Wow, so that's your girlfriend," I said. "Or at least one of them. What does the lovely Shelley make of you stalking a lady journalist?"

"You're funny."

"I try."

"And I'm not stalking her."

"No, clearly not."

Danny laughed, which made him wince again, and I felt more guilty than ever.

"She's obviously good, then," I said. "I'll have to keep a lookout for her."

"She is. I told you."

"That'll be you one day."

"Maybe. First, though, we've got to get you sorted. Will Todd be home now?"

I looked at my watch.

"What day is it? Thursday. I'm losing track. No, he should be in lectures I think. We could catch him tonight, before he goes to work."

"Okay. That works. And in the meantime we can go to the Polytechnic."

"The Polytechnic?"

"Yeah, your bit. Where the storeroom is."

"Now I know you've gone mad."

"We've got to. Find out what happened there, and we sort out everything."

"But they're never going to let me in."

"We'll worry about that when we get there."

I had significant doubts, but Danny seemed to know what he was up to. We split the bill and headed out into the cold.

Chapter 12

WITH BBC Broadcasting House just round the corner from the Polytechnic, you can often spot celebrities and pop stars, or the occasional Radio 1 DJ walking through the car park. I was slightly starstruck in my first year, but soon realised it wasn't the done thing to show excitement. That said, I was rather hoping we'd bump into someone famous just so Danny could see how cool and connected I was. I was out of luck. Danny was limping quite badly and in obvious discomfort, but to his credit, he didn't complain.

We entered the building and walked up to reception, where a familiar uniformed security man was reading a newspaper. There were lots of students milling around, and I could sense them giving me funny looks, nudging each other, and whispering my name. I took a deep breath.

"Hi Terry," I said, "can we talk to you for a moment?"

He looked up at me. We knew each other well.

"Anna, you really shouldn't be here, you know?"

"I know, I understand that, but please? Or is Sam in?"

"He's not on till later. And you definitely shouldn't be speaking to him."

"Listen, Terry, I didn't do this, okay? I know what everyone thinks. I know what it looks like, but really, honestly, it wasn't me." I pointed to Danny. "This is my friend Danny. We're just trying to find out what really happened."

"Shouldn't you be talking to the police, then?"

"They're as bad as everyone. They're blaming me, and don't seem to be looking for anyone else. But trust me, *I know* it wasn't me. Please?"

He seemed to think for a moment, then nodded.

"Come on then," he said, and indicated a doorway to the left.

We passed through to a small office out the back, out of sight of the main reception.

"I'll have to stand here so I can keep an eye on the desk," he said, "but you two take a seat."

"Thanks Terry," I said. I appreciated the show of faith, and the possible risk he was taking by even acknowledging me. Danny and I took chairs either side of a small wooden table, covered with a pile of old newspapers, an ashtray and two mugs that could have done with a serious clean.

"How can I help you, then?" he asked.

Danny took the lead.

"First of all, thanks for this, we really appreciate it."

"That's all right. I may not have long, though."

"Understood. We're just trying to find out what happened. We should probably speak to Sam really, but if you've heard anything, even if it's just gossip, it might really help."

"I've just heard what everyone's heard. Anish discovered the storeroom door smashed open, two cameras had been nicked, and the police then found them at yours." He indicated to me.

"Okay," said Danny, "but what about the actual break-in? Do they know what time it happened?"

"What? The actual minute?"

"As close as you can get."

"I don't know. All I know is that the room was locked up as normal about six so some time after that."

Danny turned to me.

"What time were you all at the restaurant?"

"Just gone eight." I started to smile, a huge sense of relief welling up inside me. "Danny! So it could have been some time between six and eight, then. Which means it could have been Todd."

My joy was short-lived.

"No, sorry," said Terry. "Sam did his rounds, checking all the doors. That was about ten, after the night classes all left. It was still locked then."

"Is he sure?"

"Cast iron. It was jemmied open. He'd have seen that."

"Shit."

"Does he keep a record of the security rounds?" asked Danny.

"There's a log book, yeah. Excuse me."

Terry moved back to the reception desk. I looked round the corner and saw him talking to a couple of students I didn't recognise. They could have been first years.

"What do you think?" I asked Danny, while we had a moment to ourselves.

"I think it sounds tricky, if I'm honest," he said. "I'd like to see the log, but if he did the round when he said he did, then it rules out Todd."

"I was so excited."

"I know, me too, but it's never that easy. What time did you leave the restaurant?"

"About half ten, maybe just after, by the time we were all on the street."

"And you got here?"

"Ten, fifteen minutes later."

"And what time did Todd take Sophie back?"

"That was right at the start. Probably half eight-ish."

"Bollocks. He couldn't have done it, then. Unless this Sam bloke's not telling the truth."

"No, he's good. I've known him since the start of last year. He's always seemed dead on."

"Sure?"

"Yeah."

Terry returned.

"Sorry about that," he said. "I'm surprised some of them are clever enough to get here with some of the questions I get. Where were we?"

"The log book?" said Danny.

"Ah yes."

Terry fetched a ring binder from the top of a filing cabinet.

"Here you go," he said, turning to a page. "It all gets initialled when he does his rounds. Anything unusual gets written down. But that night, nothing."

"Was ten o'clock the last check?" asked Danny.

"No, he'd do two-hourly rounds through the night."

"So how come he didn't spot the break-in then?"

It seemed a reasonable question to me.

"Because the later rounds are just the periphery. Checking external doors, windows, all of that. There's no need to check the stores again. Once that's all locked up, it stands to reason nobody's got access if the place is empty and nobody's broken in."

"And was the place definitely empty?"

"Definitely. Once the night classes finish, he'd go round locking rooms, then check the toilets, everything. He'd be pretty thorough."

"There's no chance he could have missed someone?"

"Not Sam, no. He's been at this too long."

I was starting to feel the whole thing was pointless. Nobody else could have done it. And yet clearly they had. But how?

Danny wasn't finished.

"You said nobody's got access to the storeroom if nobody's broken in, and yet somebody must have. Have you got any idea at all how that could have happened?"

Terry paused to think for a moment, then shook his head.

"No, sorry. The only other way would be for Sam to let someone in, if he had a visitor, but that'd get logged as well."

"And did he? That night?"

"Only Anna." He turned to me. "Sorry, love, I wish I could help you."

"You've been a big help," I said, although really it was just out of politeness. I couldn't see we were any further forward.

"I'd better be getting back," he said. "Sorry I couldn't be any more use."

We both said our thanks and then made our way back out onto the street and started walking in the general direction of the student union bar.

"It's hopeless," I said.

Danny put his arm around me.

"It's not looking good," he said.

"And you *still* believe me?"

"Anna, look me in the eyes and tell me you didn't do it."

I turned to him.

"I didn't do it," I said, the pleading evident in my voice.

"There you go then. I believe you. We'll work it out. Don't worry."

But I was worried. I was beginning to think that we'd never work out what had happened, and time was fast running out.

Chapter 13

I WASN'T sure that more alcohol would help, so I suggested going for something to eat instead. We soon found ourselves in a pizzeria, although in fairness I did then order a glass of wine, because I like it a lot, and couldn't see it would do any harm. And they give you a free one if you show them your NUS card.

"So how did you meet Todd?" Danny asked, once the food had arrived.

"It was one night in the student bar. It was a eurodisco night, I think. He was a friend of a friend and we got chatting and he asked me out. Simple as."

"I'd never have had the guts."

"Am I really that scary?"

"Not scary, just... I don't know. Unapproachable."

"Unapproachable?" I was slightly taken aback. "Why's that?"

"You were always in a big group and by far the coolest person in there."

"Really?"

"Yeah, you always looked amazing. I saw you and admired from afar."

"Now I know you're taking the piss." I paused. "God. Were you stalking me like you stalk your journalist? Shit, poor Shelley."

"You keep on about Shelley. I thought you said you weren't going to mention her if I didn't call you Paddington?"

"No, that was your love poems. Shelley fascinates me."

Danny laughed.

"Why?"

"I don't know anything about her, except she clearly doesn't exist."

"She does!"

"Have you got a picture?"

"Not on me, no."

"Well there you go then."

"Next time I see you I'll bring you a picture."

"I'll look forward to that. Still not convinced, though. I'll probably recognise which magazine it's been cut from."

"God, you're a pain."

I gave him my best confused look.

"Changing the subject," he continued, ignoring me. "Did Todd seem the jealous type?"

"Maybe, but not especially. Actually, it's weird. He stayed with me last weekend but seemed a bit off then, now I think about it. He just seemed easily irritated."

"By you? Surely not."

I didn't rise to it.

"Mainly. I couldn't do anything right. On Saturday we had a 'bring a door' party in the common room..."

"A what?"

"Bring a door. You had to take a door. Don't ask. We're students, there was drink."

Danny laughed.

"A door?"

"Yeah, room door. Cupboard. Didn't really matter."

"And why?"

"It's one of those things that seems like a good idea when you're pissed."

"I'm beginning to be glad I'm not living in halls."

"I'd have said you were missing out, until Tuesday." I sat back, momentarily overcome with a new wave of sadness. Whatever happened, the lifestyle I'd enjoyed since moving to London was never coming back.

"Anyway," I continued, eventually, "he didn't like what I was wearing so I offered to get changed and he told me not to bother."

"What were you wearing?"

"You probably already know if you've been stalking me."

"Ha! I was with Shelley last weekend, so three hundred miles away."

"On your own, then."

"I've probably still got the bus ticket."

"*Bus* ticket?"

"Non-stop Clipper. It's the cheapest way of getting back if you go up overnight."

He reached into his jacket pocket, wincing with the pain from his bruised ribs, and brought out his wallet. He started searching the compartments.

"I must have chucked it," he said, eventually.

I raised an eyebrow.

"You know what, I'm beginning to sympathise with Todd," he said, making me laugh. "Anyway, so he didn't like your outfit?"

"No, apparently my skirt was too short, which is ridiculous as it's the one I normally wear."

"I've noticed."

I raised another eyebrow.

"And I had too much make-up."

"Isn't that the point of being a goth, though? Short skirts, fishnets and lots of make-up."

"What?"

"It's like the uniform."

"No, I know what you mean, but I'll stop you there. I am *not* a goth."

"You are a bit."

"You seriously calling me a goth?"

"Not in a bad way."

"I think we need to have a proper conversation. Look at my hair. Is it black? No. Purple? No. Is it all lovely and luxuriant? Admittedly not today, but generally? Yes. Do I always wear black?"

"Yes."

"Granted. But the answer you're looking for is no. So no, not a goth. Although I do like The Cure, but that's just a coincidence."

"I believe you. Although you do wear fishnets."

"Oooh. Anyway, yes, he didn't like the skirt, didn't like the make-up and wasn't interested in sex if you want to get graphic about things."

"Prefer not to. Bordering on too much detail."

"I thought that as I said it."

Danny smiled. "In any case, he'd squash you. So something was up then?"

"Seems like it, with the benefit of hindsight. It didn't really occur to me at the time. I just thought he was stressed, maybe. Anyway, we had an okay weekend apart from that, and when he went back on Sunday I thought it was all back to normal. I just put it down to one of those things."

"And he was okay on the Monday?"

"Yeah, although I suppose no, not really. He asked me to go back home with him but I said I couldn't. And then as soon as Sophie got ill he was off like the proverbial. Didn't make any attempt to come back. He just said he'd see me at the weekend."

Danny called the waiter and asked for the bill before continuing.

"I don't want to annoy you because I know he was your boyfriend, but everything I've heard makes me not like the bloke."

"I'm coming round to that way of thinking. And that's before he beat you up."

"If it was him."

"I know but it sounds like it. So what now, Danny?"

He looked at his watch.

"Will he be home yet?"

"Possibly. If not, then probably by the time we get there."

"Come on then. Let's see what he can tell us."

I really wasn't sure about this, but I was running out of options.

We weren't there long.

I knocked on the door, Todd eventually answered, then started laughing when he saw us. We weren't invited in, although I didn't expect to be. He denied having been anywhere near the hall of residence the previous night, but seemed to find Danny's pain amusing. No, apparently, he didn't know anything about it. Yes, apparently we could fuck off also. And then he slammed the door.

"Do you reckon it was him?" I asked as we set off back to the bus stop.

"Ninety-nine point nine percent definite. Did you see his hand and the broken skin on his knuckles? I think I could see bits of my face still in it."

"Bastard."

"Are you always this adept at choosing boyfriends?"

"I'm utterly shit at it." We arrived at the bus stop and I sat down on the bench at the back of the shelter. "Every one of them's been a disaster. I'm going to give up."

"You can't give up yet. You've just got to find the right one."

"But all the good ones have gone. And anyway, it's never that simple, is it?"

"Oh God. I'm going to wish I hadn't asked."

"It's just guaranteed to end in tears."

"Is it?"

"Of course it is." In the distance I could see the warm yellow glow of an approaching bus. I didn't know if it was ours. I had no idea where we were going. Danny joined me on the bench.

"In what way?" he asked.

"It's just blindingly obvious. Do you like one night stands?"

"Wow, are you offering?"

"No, and that's the point. They're shit, getting pawed by some drunken adolescent who's more interested in my legs than my name. Why would you even bother? It's like the relationship equivalent of going to McDonald's."

"Really?"

"Yes. And falling in love and lifelong commitment is like fine dining at a Michelin-starred restaurant."

The bus got closer but neither of us moved. There'd be another one along shortly anyway.

"Okay," said Danny.

"But when you first meet somebody you know nothing about them, so how do you know you're going to be compatible long term?"

"You don't. That's why you go on dates and get to know them."

"Exactly!"

I could sense Danny looking at me, but I refused to meet his eyes.

"I'm failing to see the problem, then," he said.

"Oh Danny. Do you not get it?"

"Get what?"

"What's in between the two extremes? That's like going to a

nice restaurant, kind of a mid-priced sort of place. Good menu, decent food. And you go there a lot, but they're not too hot on hygiene. So one day, eventually, inevitably, you've got a whole spectrum of heartache, because the whole thing, by definition, is going to end in an unpleasant mess."

"Right."

"Frankly it's not worth the trouble. As we've very much seen this week. The whole thing is fundamentally flawed."

The bus stopped. A couple of passengers got off, but we didn't move.

"How old are you?" Danny asked as it departed.

"Nineteen."

"And you don't think you might meet somebody, one day, who starts out as a standard kind of middle-ground relationship, but then as you get to know them, feelings develop and suddenly it becomes a lifelong thing?"

"No, because as I quite clearly remember pointing out, all the good ones have, in fact, already gone. Look at you. Seem like a nice bloke - pact or not, I think I'm allowed to say that - but obviously Shelley's already planted the flag, as it were. Albeit she doesn't exist."

I paused to look at him to see if there was any reaction. Annoyingly, he just seemed to be humouring me and didn't speak.

"Anyway, where now?" I continued. "Seriously, I'm giving up on the whole thing, so unless we've got a better plan I should probably just go home where everybody hates me, and then stay in my room, crying until my eyes run out of tears, and wait for the executioner to come knocking."

Danny reached for my hand. I moved to lean in towards him, and rested my head on his shoulder. He put his arm around me and pulled me close. I tried to be sensitive to his bruises.

"We're not giving up," he said. "And I've been thinking about you going home."

"Can't wait to get shot of me?"

Another bus was approaching.

"No. Thinking you should come to stay with me."

"Do what?"

"Come and stay with me. Just till this all gets sorted. You can have my room and I'll go on the sofa. The others won't mind, there's always hangers-on about the place."

"Danny, I..." I shook my head. "I couldn't. I've caused you enough trouble already."

"Are you always going to be like this?"

"Like what?"

"Forget it. Look, I wouldn't have offered if I didn't want you to do it. I do. So will you come?"

"I don't know what to say." It didn't take me long to assess the options. I looked up at his kind eyes and wanted to lose myself within them.

"Yes," I said eventually. "I'd love to."

"Brilliant. It's done then. Let's pop back to yours and get an overnight bag, then I'll introduce you to the delights of Kentish Town."

"Are you sure?"

"Yes, come on."

The bus stopped. We got on, Danny holding my hand. To anyone else we must have looked like two young lovers, but I was having feelings the likes of which I'd never felt before.

Chapter 14

I F there was one advantage to Danny's injuries, it was that he didn't fancy all of the stairs and escalators of the Underground, so he accepted my suggestion of getting the bus from the hall of residence back to Kentish Town. Obviously it would have been insensitive to declare this as the upside of him taking a beating, so I kept quiet. However, as I sat next to him on the journey through Camden, I perhaps snuggled in a bit more closely than Shelley would have appreciated.

The streets were vaguely familiar. I'd been here once to buy some Dr. Martens shoes from a shop just by Camden Town station, and I'd had a couple of memorable nights at the Camden Palace in my first year in London. But Kentish Town itself, which lay just beyond, was unfamiliar territory, and as Danny led me up the stairs to his Victorian terraced house, I was beginning to lose my bearings.

He opened the door and flicked a light switch as we entered the high-ceilinged hallway. Nothing happened.

"That's typical," he said. "Leave your bag here and I'll introduce you to the others."

Danny led the way, ignoring the first two doors, and then past an impressive-looking staircase. I hadn't given much thought to his housemates. The door at the end led to the kitchen, where a man with a beard and scruffy hair was sitting on a bench that ran alongside a wooden table, rolling something that looked suspiciously like a joint.

"Anna, meet Wedge. Wedge, Anna," said Danny.

Wedge?

"Cool man, you bagged a goth chick," said Wedge, who stood up, offered me his hand to shake, and then bowed as I accepted.

"Pleased to meet you," I said, "though technically not a goth."

"Hey, you're cool, you be whoever you wanna be."

"Anna's come to stay for a bit," Danny continued. "Is Gary in?"

"In his room, man. Anna, come and sit next to the Wedge." He moved along the bench and patted the space next to him.

I gave Danny a look, but he just raised an eyebrow. In for a pound.

"What's happened to the hall light?" he asked.

"Big bang, man. I pressed the switch and... boof! We shall embrace the darkness."

"Fair dos," said Danny, who then turned to me. "Cup of tea? Or something stronger?"

"I never say no to tea, normally. But stronger's good."

"White wine?"

"Perfect."

Wedge raised his can of Red Stripe.

"Not for me, I'm spoken for," he said. "So, Anna, where have you come from, and how come my man Danny's been hiding you? If you were with the Wedge I'd be putting up posters to tell the world."

"You're very kind," I said. "We met at the bar but it's a kind of long story. So, er, Wedge, are you a student?"

"Student of life, man. And he's moving you in already? The Danster is an operator."

"Not really moving in, just staying for a bit while I sort a couple of things out."

"You can stay as long as you like, babe. We always have room for beautiful ladies."

I couldn't work him out. Seventies throwback or just stoned? I suspected the latter. Danny reached into the fridge for a bottle. It was a gift-wrapped opportunity.

"You make it sound like Danny brings a lot of girls home. Am I just the latest of many?" I asked.

"The Wedge does not divulge secrets, man." He turned to Danny. "She's checking up on you. She's keen." He laughed, but the laugh turned into a cough. He lit the joint, then offered it to me, but I declined. "What are your troubles, young beautiful Anna? I shall make them all go away."

"That's another long story," I said. "But go on, tell me all about Danny and his girlfriends. I'd love to know."

"Wine's ready," said Danny, putting a glass down in front of me, clearly keen to change the subject. He sat down opposite, and gave me a warning look. Wedge stood up.

"I shall leave you two to gel," he said. "Later, people."

"So that was Wedge, then?" I said once he was out of the room. "Seems nice." I chuckled.

"He's a character. Useless at paying his rent, though."

"And who's the other? Gary?"

"Yeah, Gary's kind of the polar opposite. He's like a super-fit athlete."

"Ooh, I like the sound of him already."

"I'd better make sure he stays out of the way, then. Cheers." Danny raised his glass and we did the chink thing.

"Thanks for this," I said. "And for looking after me. I know I keep saying it."

"My pleasure. I suggest we get pissed and see if everything looks clearer with a hangover."

"You're not going to use alcohol as an excuse to make some sort of drunken pass at me?"

"As if. Told you, we've got an agreement."

"That's a shame. You could, though, now we're here, show me some of your pictures of Shelley. Maybe read some of her poems."

"God, you are relentless. Let's go to the front room. I'll bring the bottle."

And so the evening developed. It was just what I needed to take my mind off things. A few miles away, it transpired, the police were searching for me, having come to arrest me, but we were oblivious.

We curled up together on the sofa and talked and talked. I revealed my wayward past, bunking off school to take pictures for a local newspaper (on the good days) or bunking off school to stay at home and drink Country Manor (the bad). I told Danny things I'd never told anyone before, including about my parents, and my mum's less-than-wholehearted support for my photographic endeavours. Danny told me about his Sunderland days, and afternoons in the fog at Roker Park, or walking along deserted beaches planning his assault on the pop charts. He played me a demo tape he'd recorded when it looked like his band was going places. It was surprisingly good. I was genuinely impressed.

At one point Gary appeared. I saw what Danny meant. He had an incredible physique. And two girlfriends, apparently, which seemed to be causing issues that he explained at length, much to Danny's amusement. A second bottle of wine appeared, which Gary shared, and then Danny said he had to pop out for a moment, and returned with a delicious-looking Indian takeaway, along with a third bottle. It was like a magic trick. By the time we'd done justice to the last of the wine, I was having difficulty speaking and borderline fancying a fag, but didn't want to tarnish my reputation any further on that score.

It was just past midnight when Danny showed me up to his

room. He was as good as his word. I collapsed onto the wonderful double bed while he said he would take the sofa, back downstairs. I thought about telling him he could stay with me, but it wouldn't have been right. Not in those circumstances, while drink could be blamed for making us both do something that either one of us might regret. Why risk a friendship for something you probably wouldn't remember anyway?

It occurred to me that he still hadn't shown me any pictures of Shelley, but I didn't want to search his room for evidence of her existence. That would have been a breach of trust, and Danny deserved much better. But lying there, in his bed, looking at his ceiling, I had a feeling of calm that I'd been denied for the last few days, and passed into a deep, restorative sleep. If only I could have stayed there forever.

Chapter 15

Friday, November 24th, 1989

WHEN I finally surfaced, the sense of slight disorientation was soon replaced by a crushing headache. The third bottle of wine had definitely been an error, Gary's assistance or not. I may have been an expert on the futility of relationships, but I still had much to learn about my body's ability to process alcohol.

I heard a door bang downstairs. I edged carefully out of bed, leant against the wall for support, and pulled back the edge of the curtain. The daylight was almost blinding. Wedge was on the path downstairs, mounting a bicycle. I saw him pedal off, on the road, against the flow of the traffic.

Danny was already in the kitchen, fully dressed, when I eventually made it downstairs.

"Speak quietly," I said as I walked into the room.

"How are you feeling?"

I doubt I was looking my best. I hadn't been in the shower, my make-up was non-existent, and my hair almost certainly looked electrified. Danny didn't seem to recoil too badly, though, which was encouraging.

"Tender. You?"

"Been better. Did you sleep well?"

"Actually brilliantly. You have a very comfortable bed."

"Did you dribble on my pillow?"

"Quite possibly, but I dread to think what you get up to in there, so we're probably even."

I took a seat at the kitchen table, and then felt guilty when Danny got up and offered to make me tea and toast.

"How are the injuries?" I asked.

"Sore. I've got ibuprofens if you want some."

"Just pass the whole packet. Actually, a glass of water would be good."

I took the glass and swallowed the tablets, hoping they'd kick in quickly.

"Did you have any moment of clarity overnight?" I asked, once the toast was served and Danny had rejoined me.

"No, not really," he said. "I keep going over things in my mind, but there are bits I just don't understand."

"Such as?"

"All of it really."

"I know that feeling."

"I've got aspirations to be an investigative journalist, and yet frankly I think I'm useless."

"Don't be hard on yourself. If nothing else you've made the last few days bearable. It's been brilliant getting to know you. Even if I'm going to be sent to Holloway imminently and I'll never see you again."

"It won't come to that."

"I wouldn't count on it."

"It won't, honestly. Even if they can persuade a court you did it, you're looking at a fine. They're not going to bang you up for a first offence of two cameras."

"But they keep talking about a whole load of other stuff. As far as I know, I'm a serial burglar. I may have a warehouse full of nicked equipment and God knows what else. I'm a walking crimewave."

"Well, if they charge you, at least it'll give us something else to look into."

"It's pointless, though. I may as well face it. I'm fucked."

I looked at Danny, wondering what he really thought of me. I'd made my problem his problem, but really he had better things to be doing with his life. Student protests or not, he was missing lectures because of me. He'd been beaten up because of me. And what did I have to give him in return?

"If you ever get your band back together I'll do some pictures for you," I said, at last, clutching at straws.

"That's not going to happen. But thank you."

He reached across the table to me and gave my hand a squeeze.

"You've got lovely hands," he said. "I especially like the black nail varnish."

I laughed. "Are you doing the goth thing again?"

"As if."

"Oh Danny, it's all a bloody mess. I just want to wind the clock back and start this week all over again. Everything was going so well up until Monday, apart from Todd being a pain in the arse. I'd spent all day in my room, writing an essay on colours and music, and then it just all fell apart. Everything was fine, then bang!"

Danny let go of my hand.

"Say that again," he said.

"Say what again?"

"What you just said."

"Something about wanting to start the week all over again."

"That'll do. And winding the clock back. And Todd."

"Something like that. Why?"

"I'm going to have to go and talk to somebody. Wait here till I get back."

"Where are you going?"

"Back to the Polytechnic. I think I know how they've done it."

"What? Tell me."

"No, you'll think I'm mad. I just need to check something. I'll be as quick as I can."

And then he was gone.

Chapter 16

DANNY ran up the escalator at Oxford Circus as best as his injuries would allow, then pushed his way through the crowds on Regent Street, on his way to the Polytechnic building. Timing could be vital, and there wasn't a minute to lose.

"Hi again," he said to Terry at the reception desk. "Sorry to bother you, but I need to speak to the person in charge of the storeroom."

Terry gave a look of immediate recognition.

"You'll need to sign in," he said. He passed Danny a pen. "Third floor. Lift's through the double doors. Ask for Anish."

"Thank you, you're a star."

Danny took the lift with two other students. When they got out at the same floor, he asked them for directions. Moments later he was standing at a wooden counter, beyond which was a room with shelves full of equipment. There was evidence of recent repairs to the door frame.

"Hi," he said to the man in the lab coat behind the desk. "Are you Anish?"

"I am. And you are?"

"Danny Churchill." He showed his student ID card. "I'm from a different faculty but I wonder if I can ask you a couple of questions?"

"About cameras?"

"About the break-in."

Ten minutes later he was back outside, and dialling a number from the callbox opposite the Polytechnic building, desperately hoping she'd pick up.

She did.

"Anna, quick question," he said. "When did Todd last stay with you?"

"I told you. Last Saturday."

"And he stayed in your room."

"Yeah, Friday and Saturday night."

"And you had the party in the common room on Saturday?"

"We did."

"And whose idea was it?"

"I'm not sure. One of the girls, I think."

"Perfect."

"Danny, what is going on?"

"Stay there. I think I've nailed it. I'm heading back now."

He replaced the handset and clenched his fist in celebration.

Chapter 17

I HAD no idea what Danny was up to, but when he returned to the house he had a huge smile. He gave me a hug and kissed me on the forehead.

"What's going on, Poirot?" I asked.

He told me. And I couldn't quite believe the treachery.

We called the police and arranged to meet them at the hall of residence at 5pm. They seemed keen. There was a warrant for my arrest. But if Danny was right, and I had absolutely no reason to doubt him, then I had nothing more to fear. I'd been carrying the weight of suspicion, of doubt and failure, and complete lack of comprehension. But now everything made sense, within the context of nothing really making sense at all. The rank deviousness astonished me.

Suddenly I felt free. I wanted to stand on a rooftop and shout "Bastards!" into the breeze, hoping my voice would carry, specifically to Todd and those who had doubted me. This was my moment. Our moment. I would have been lost without Danny. Who knows what my life would have become? I wanted to put everything behind me and move on, but at the same time, I knew that the experiences and the bond formed with Danny over the last few days would shape my life forever.

I made sure I was looking my best, although now, looking back, there was a hint of vampire. We perhaps made an unlikely couple as we boarded the lift to the eighth floor. Sophie and Amelia were in the common room as we passed. I saw them look at us. I heard my name. Good. Let them talk about me. Let them say whatever they wanted. I looked forward to seeing their faces soon.

The police came just before five. There was a knock at the door. The same two detectives were there: DS Phil Matthews and DC Gordon Kendrick. They didn't look pleased to see me, but for once I was very pleased to see them.

"Come in," I said. "Have a chair, sit on the bed, wherever really. Would you like a cup of tea?"

DC Kendrick spoke: "Anna Burgin, I'm arresting you in connection with the theft of photographic equipment..."

"Can I stop you there?" said Danny.

"And you are?" asked the detective, noticing him for the first time.

"Danny Churchill. I'm a friend of Anna's. And if you can just give us two minutes of your time, I can tell you what really happened. Trust me. We can clear this all up in an instant and you can arrest the person who's actually responsible."

He looked at his colleague, who shrugged, then nodded. Both were still standing.

"Go on, then. Two minutes and not a second more," he said.

"Okay," Danny began. I looked at him and smiled. I was desperately proud. "We all know the facts, the storeroom was broken into, and the cameras were found in Anna's room. But it wasn't Anna who put them there. Her boyfriend - ex-boyfriend - stayed with her the previous Saturday."

"And you're saying he put them there?" asked DC Kendrick. "Two days before they were stolen?"

"No, he didn't. He's not a nice bloke, and I really wanted to believe he had, but Anna swears he couldn't have done. The bag he turned up with wasn't big enough to conceal them, and she was with him pretty much every minute of the whole weekend."

"Right - well, this isn't getting us anywhere."

"But I'll tell you who did."

The policeman sighed.

"Go on."

"One of the other students. She's out there now. You'll see her in the common room. You can't miss her. Bright red hair. Her name's Sophie. Sophie Webb. And if you look in her room, I suspect you'll also find some of the other things you're looking for."

"Sorry, Danny, or whatever your name is, you're wasting our time."

"I'm not, trust me."

"Look, we know Sophie. We've spoken to her. She didn't go anywhere near the Polytechnic that night. She was here, ill. The lad Jason gave her an alibi."

"I know. And I agree. She wasn't there."

"Jesus." He looked at his colleague, who nodded. "Right, I've heard enough of this. Ms Burgin, you're coming with us."

"But I can tell you how she did it," said Danny.

The policeman stopped and turned towards him, assessing for a moment.

"Go on."

"Okay. The cameras weren't stolen when the break-in happened. The break-in was a decoy. The cameras were already here. I spoke to Anish at the storeroom and he confirmed everything."

The detectives looked at each other then both sat down on the bed.

"Go on," said DC Kendrick again.

"We had a party on Saturday night," I said, feeling it was time to add my input. "We all had to take a door. I know that sounds stupid but it seemed funny at the time. I took the door off my wardrobe."

"And you're saying that's when she put the cameras in? That's not possible, because they were signed out in use at the Polytechnic on Monday morning."

"I know," said Danny, "but it's when Sophie got the idea. She knocked on Anna's door to tell her that the party was starting. When Anna opened the door, Sophie would have been able to see straight into her wardrobe."

"It was never the tidiest," I confessed. "There were clothes piled up on the bottom."

"We noticed."

Danny continued.

"On Monday, as you say, the cameras were signed out in the morning but returned and signed back in on Monday afternoon. I checked with Anish at the storeroom. But he also told me that Sophie had been to see him that afternoon, just before closing time, complaining of feeling unwell."

"She was ill that night at the restaurant too," I added. "Todd had to bring her home."

"The fact is," said Danny, "she wasn't ill at all. She asked Anish to get her a glass of water. Crucially, therefore, she was alone for perhaps a minute. The cameras had just been signed back in, and were still out on one of the returns shelves, waiting to be put away. That's when she stole them, slipped them straight into her bag. Anish returned with the glass, then sat with her for a few minutes. It was the end of the day. He decided he'd sort out the equipment in the morning. He locked up and then walked her down to reception to make sure she was okay."

"As far as he was concerned, the cameras were in there when he locked the door," I added.

"Okay," said DS Matthews. "But how come they still ended up in your room? Why would she do that? And who broke into the storeroom?"

"This is where she's tried to be clever," said Danny. "She staged the break-in to make it look like it happened overnight, but I'll come on to that. As you know, it's not the first time things have gone missing. I think she realised things were heating up and you'd be investigating. So she hid the cameras in Anna's room and made sure you'd find them, so you'd then pin everything on Anna. She'd lose those two but it was a small sacrifice to have the blame for all the thefts shift onto someone else."

"And how did she get them in there?"

"On Monday night, Amelia came and asked me if I'd like to go to dinner with them," I said. "I popped down the corridor to the bathroom to, well, freshen up, before setting off."

"Which means Anna's room was unlocked for about two minutes," Danny continued. "Sophie seized her chance, and stuffed the cameras under the clothes while Anna was in the bathroom. Then all she had to do was make it look like Anna was the only possible suspect by making sure she was in the Polytechnic building that night."

"She pretended to be ill at the restaurant," I said. "She's on my course so she asked me to pick up some books from her locker for her. She said she wouldn't be in the next day."

"But she was," said Danny. "She got down there first thing. One of the others from here, Jason, went with her. Anish normally gets in first but they got there about a minute before. I checked with Terry. She raced up to the storeroom and jemmied it open with a screwdriver then hid in the stairwell. Anish turned up a few seconds later, having been delayed by Jason, and noticed the door. He confirmed Sophie was the first person to arrive straight after."

"She pretended to be shocked," I added, "and said it must

have happened overnight. He didn't have any reason to doubt her. He'd seen her arrive in reception just before he did. She didn't have a bag, and even if she had, she hadn't had time to break in, find things and steal them. She only just had time to break the door."

"Jason didn't realise he was involved," continued Danny. "His only part in this was to ask Anish something to delay him a moment at Sophie's request. Once Anish got upstairs, he confirmed Sophie came from the stairwell. He remembers now, and said it seemed odd at the time, but he hadn't given it a second thought in all the shock of finding the break-in. The stairs are right by the lift, but nobody ever takes the stairs, especially to go up."

"And after that, she came straight back here, and went back to pretending to be ill," I said, in conclusion. "But to go back to what Danny said earlier, if you go and look in her room, we think you'll find some of the other things you've been looking for. Unless she's already sold them."

The two detectives looked at each other.

"And she's been stealing stuff off this floor for ages, too. She used this as an opportunity to pin all that on me. That's why everybody hates me."

"Which one's her room?" asked DC Kendrick, after a moment.

"802," I said. "Two doors down."

Chapter 18

THERE was something strangely therapeutic about seeing Danny proved right and watching Sophie being taken away in a police car instead of me, but I still felt the whole thing was so terribly sad. It transpired she did have a violent dealer to pay, and when the police asked to inspect her room she broke down in tears. It wasn't long before she confessed to everything. I heard later, from Jason, that she'd also had her eye on Todd, so getting me out of the way would have other benefits there. I couldn't see that happening now, but if it did, they're welcome to each other.

I took Danny out for yet another meal, but this time to celebrate. I booked a table in a small restaurant, close to his house in Kentish Town. I wanted to thank him, not just for all of his hard work, but mainly for being the only person who believed in me, even when I'd started doubting myself.

"I still think it was Todd that beat you up," I said as we waited for the food to arrive.

"Unquestionably," he said. "But I think he was just jealous. He'd obviously seen us talking together and got the wrong end of it - especially if you'd not been getting on."

"Are you going to press charges?"

Danny shook his head.

"There's no point. I couldn't prove it. But he knows, and we know. I think he'll leave us alone now."

"One thing does bother me, though." I found it hard to suppress a smile.

"What's that?"

"I spent a whole evening at your house, and still haven't seen any actual evidence of the existence of the mysterious Shelley. Not even a single line of verse."

"God, not this again." Danny laughed. "Okay, I'll make a confession."

"She doesn't exist! Ha! I knew it."

"No, she's coming down for the weekend. She's very keen to meet you. Actually, I left a note with Gary to tell her where we were, so she could come to meet us here."

As if on cue, the restaurant door opened. A statuesque young woman with gorgeous blonde hair, looking about as far removed from me as possible, looked over in our direction. Danny waved. She started approaching. I suddenly felt very small indeed.

"Oh fuck," I said. Danny just winked. He stood up.

"I'll make introductions," he said. I stood as well, not quite knowing what to do with myself, but feeling excruciatingly embarrassed. I'd lost my heart to her boyfriend, pact or not. I'd slept in his bed. I'd doubted everything about her, and yet here she was.

"You must be Anna," she said, before Danny had a chance to speak. "I've heard a lot about you."

"And me you likewise," I said, offering my hand for her to shake. I was overcome by guilt.

"Really?" she said. "That's odd."

I could see Danny's face cracking up.

"Anna," he said. "I'd like to introduce you to Jill. Gary's girlfriend."

"Oh," I said.

"I'm not stopping," she continued, giving me a funny look. "I'm just passing on a message. Shelley phoned and said her bus is running about two hours late, but she'll see you this evening. And the landlord's been round again. Wedge still hasn't paid his rent. Apparently if he doesn't clear the backlog by Monday you're all getting evicted."

"Shit, I thought that would happen," said Danny.

"Anyway, I'll leave you to it, Maybe see you later?"

Danny nodded. She turned and left us to it.

"You enjoyed that," I said. "Bastard."

Danny reached across and held my hand. I didn't try to stop him.

"Seriously, it still hurts to laugh," he said. "Your face, though..."

Luckily, the waiter turned up before I had the chance to respond.

Chapter 19

The final years

I DID get to meet Shelley eventually. She wasn't at all like I'd expected. She was lovely in her own way, but quite quiet at first. I think I made her nervous. She was pretty too, annoyingly, in a classically fresh-faced girl-next-door kind of a way. But then as we got to know each other, over the course of the evening, she warmed up and I began to see her smile. She had irritatingly perfect teeth, too.

Danny and Shelley escorted me back to my hall of residence, but didn't take me up on my offer of tea. I suspect they had better things to be getting home to, having not seen each other for nearly a week. But what a week it had been.

Amelia and Sara were in the kitchen when I arrived on the eighth floor. They both tried to apologise, and I accepted with reasonably good grace, but I knew things would never return to normal. Jason apologised too. He was mortified that he had been an unwitting accomplice. He'd only gone with Sophie because he was convinced she was ill, and he was desperately keen to make sure she was looked after.

Over the weekend, I had a lot of time to myself, and decided to make fundamental changes. I'd start by looking for somewhere new to live for next term. It was time to leave the security of the hall, and branch out on my own.

I didn't see Danny all weekend and missed him terribly. I was suffering from the agonising effects of a crush, made worse by my imagination conjuring up all sorts of unwanted imagery about what might be happening in his lovely double bed. My heart leapt when he phoned me on Monday evening, asking if I'd like to meet for a drink. I knew that if I accepted I'd be fooling myself, but I did so anyway. I'll never learn.

"So how was your weekend," I asked, once we were together. "Shelley get home okay?"

"She did, yes. And it was good, thank you. Lots of fun after a stressful week."

"Are you using the word fun as a euphemism?"

"Euphemism for what?"

I gave him a look.

"Actually, don't tell me. It's best I don't know."

"How were things in the hall?" he asked, changing the subject. I kind of did want to know, but only to confirm that they hadn't been up to anything. That wasn't going to happen.

"Frosty. I've had a lot of thinking time. I'm going to move out after Christmas. God knows where, but it's time."

"Don't even start me. We've just been evicted."

"No!"

"Yup. Wedge owed three months and the landlord lost it. He's giving us to the end of term but then we've got to go, too."

"Could he not just evict Wedge?"

"It's all three of us on the same contract. He's had it with students, apparently. He's going for young professionals as supposedly they 'treat the place with more respect', which basically means they have the money to pay the rent on time."

"Shit. I'm sorry to hear all that. What'll you do?"

"Look to find somewhere new. It's all we can do."

"Well, if you need a new flatmate, let me know."

I said that before I'd really had time to think about it, but as time moved on, that's exactly what happened. We started sharing house-hunting stories, until, in the end, we both came across the same place, in Chalk Farm, sharing with four other students. It wasn't far from either Camden or Danny's old place and it was perfect. We moved in together - albeit in separate rooms - the following January. Our friendship, based on mutual respect and my undying devotion, has only prospered ever since.

Shelley came to stay for a few weekends until the inevitable messy break-up. I told Danny he should have listened to me, but he was inconsolable for a while, and I don't think my hard-earned sageness helped. That said, I tried a few more disastrous dalliances of my own, but they rarely progressed beyond the invitation-to-dinner, back-for-coffee, what-on-earth-was-I-thinking next morning stage.

In general, though, it was a good period. Ever more of my free time was taken up helping Mark Colby at his photographic studio, learning all about the techniques and business of high-end fashion photography.

I went from tea girl to lighting assistant, and then, when he went on glamorous foreign trips, he started to trust me enough to let me use his equipment to build my own portfolio. My friend Colette was an aspiring model, so we worked together, exploring ideas, experimenting with sets, outfits and lighting, until I began to develop a style of my own. There was huge excitement when one of our shoots was accepted by an underground fashion magazine. Colette went on to be a star, and I've done okay. When I graduated, I set up my own studio and called it Passion Fruit, partly because I wanted to make sensual, passionate images, and partly as a nod to my first paid commission of a supermarket's fruit bowl. I'm now reasonably in demand, although it's a hugely competitive industry and you can never afford to stop learning.

Danny's wish came true when he finally got to meet his idol, Clare Woodbrook from the Daily Echo. She was booked as a guest lecturer in his final year. God - I've rarely seen him so excited.

He was up ridiculously early to make sure he'd be there first, desperate to bag a front row seat in the lecture theatre. He'd prepared dozens of questions for the inevitable Q&A, which I suspect just irritated all the other students, who would have been much more interested in getting to the bar.

At the end, he told me he'd hung around to introduce himself, and apparently - perhaps out of some kindred spirit of northern-ness - she was only too happy to chat. In the end they went to the college canteen where she bought him a cup of tea, before giving him her office number and an open invitation to visit her building on Fleet Street to see her in action.

That was it, then. He was deeply in love, although I don't think he was ever brave enough to tell her - or me - in quite as many words. It's the same old thing really: why risk what you have for something else that may be unattainable. I'm sure there's a proverb about that. Something to do with a dog with a bone in its mouth, seeing its reflection in a river, and opening its mouth to catch the reflection, but losing the real bone in the process. Sometimes I think I should be the writer, haha.

Clare became Danny's mentor. They kept in touch throughout the rest of his final year, and I'd often get bored, hearing him bang on about how much she'd taught him. Not that I'm the jealous type, obviously, but really? At least Mark, who was fulfilling a similar role for me, had the forethought to be gay. To Clare's credit, she was as good as her word, and when Danny graduated she offered him a full-time job, as her researcher.

Before I knew it, they were going out to swanky awards dos

together and he was flying off on research trips, hunting down master fraudsters. He loved the job, and I was very pleased for him, and proud when I saw his name in print. I met Clare a couple of times, and even offered her my photographic skills, but I don't think she took me seriously.

By the start of 1993, both Danny and I were building up our careers. We moved to a new flat for just the two of us, in Rochester Square in Camden. Our friendship was deeper than ever, built on mutual trust, admiration, and understanding. I hoped those days would never end. But then one morning Clare arranged to meet Danny for lunch. She didn't turn up, and her car was found abandoned on the M25. And that was the day everything changed.

The End.

FEEL FREE TO SAY HELLO… :-)

If you enjoyed the book, have any queries, or just want to say hello, I'd love to hear from you via www.davidbradwell.com.

You can also follow me on Twitter: @dbshq - or see what Anna is up to: @AnnaBurginNW1

If you enjoyed In The Frame, you should read **Cold Press** - book 1 in the Anna Burgin series.

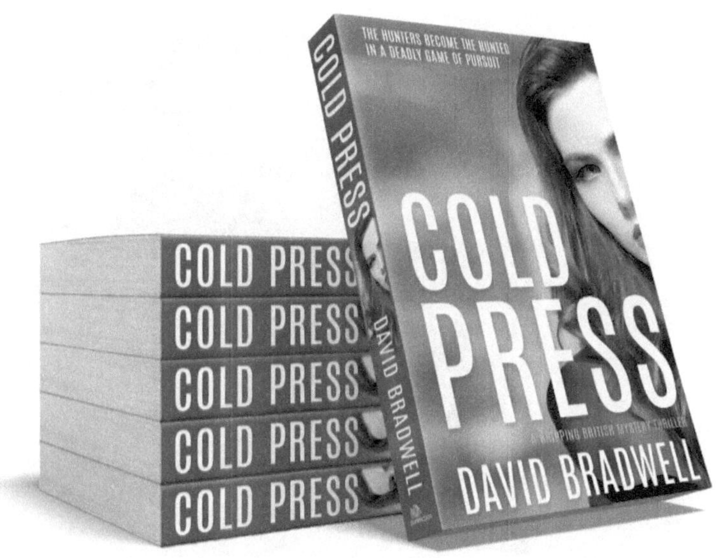

London. 1993. Investigative journalist Clare Woodbrook goes missing on the brink of unveiling her biggest-ever story. Is it kidnap? Murder?

Worse still, the police investigation into her disappearance is being headed up by a corrupt DCI - himself the subject of one of Clare's current investigations.

Clare's researcher Danny Churchill sets out to find her, and enlists the help of his flatmate - feisty fashion photographer Anna Burgin. But they soon realise that nobody can be trusted. And as the search becomes ever more desperate, suddenly their own lives are very much on the line.

Packed with intrigue, twists, conspiracies, and dark humour, Cold Press is a hugely entertaining British thriller, with a sting in the tail.

Also available: **Out Of the Red** - book 2 in the Anna Burgin
series

The gripping, twist-filled sequel to Cold Press.

Investigative journalist Danny Churchill is hot on the trail of
Graham March - the disgraced former police DCI. The
investigation takes him to Germany where he soon starts to
uncover dark secrets and new depths of depravity.

Back in London, and aided by his flatmate - fashion photographer
Anna Burgin - Danny's investigation intensifies, but as he gets
closer to the truth, the body count starts to rise.

*Help is offered from the most unlikely of sources, but if Danny
accepts, is he doing a deal with the devil herself?*

The sequel to Out Of The Red is book 4: **Fade To Silence.**

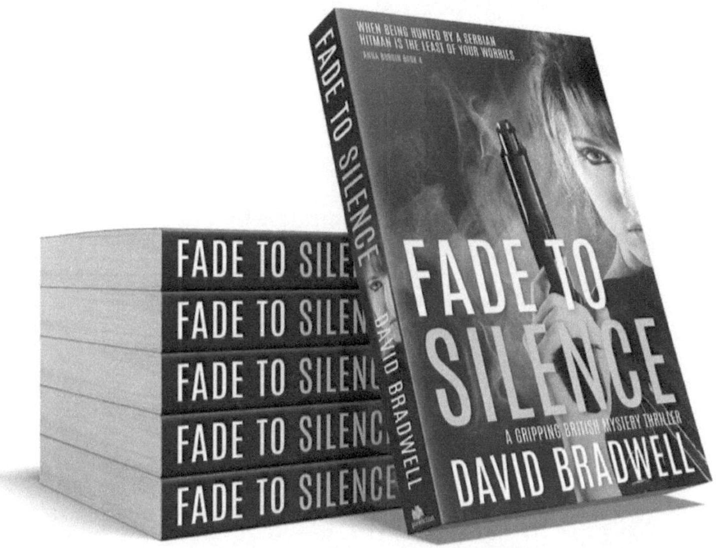

You know you've got problems when being hunted by a Serbian hitman is the least of your worries...

Balkan gangsters, corporate spies and a fugitive killer are all on the loose in London, but when a body shows up, all of the evidence points to the victim's wife.

Journalist Danny Churchill wants to find the truth. But when reports emerge of a huge shipment of weapons heading to the UK, it soon becomes the most dangerous and action-packed investigation so far.

Packed with twists, intrigue and dark humour, Fade To Silence is book 4 in the bestselling Anna Burgin series.

www.ingramcontent.com/pod-product-compliance
Lightning Source LLC
Chambersburg PA
CBHW021739190726
48288CB00009B/3103